Lanier was about to walk toward the hotel when her heart began racing…

The hair on the back of her neck stood to attention, and her hearing became sensitive to sound—any sound.

She glanced around, one hand on her gun. A warning voice whispered in her head. Someone was watching her—Lanier could almost feel their angry gaze.

The sound of a vehicle door closing captured her attention. She spotted a lone man walking to the front entrance. He never once looked her way.

Lanier bit her bottom lip and forced her body to relax. Her watcher was still out there somewhere hidden in the shadows, his body merged into the ominous silhouettes of the buildings dotted along the street. Lanier knew he wanted her to know he was there. Her fear gave him power.

I'm not afraid of you was the message she wanted to send with her body language. Her gaze was trained on the reflective glass across the front of the building. If there was movement of any kind, she'd be more than ready…

Books by Jacquelin Thomas

Love Inspired Cold Case

Evidence Uncovered

Harlequin Heartwarming

A Family for the Firefighter
Her Hometown Hero
Her Marine Hero

Visit the Author Profile page
at LoveInspired.com for more titles.

EVIDENCE UNCOVERED

JACQUELIN THOMAS

LOVE INSPIRED
INSPIRATIONAL ROMANCE

To my mother and my first heartbeat, Bevin.
There are no words to describe my loss since
our Heavenly Father welcomed you home.
However, I have a measure of peace
in knowing that you are in His care.
I hope you know that I will love you both forever.

LOVE INSPIRED®
INSPIRATIONAL ROMANCE

PLEASE RECYCLE
THIS PRODUCT IS RECYCLABLE

Recycling programs
for this product may
not exist in your area.

ISBN-13: 978-1-335-42612-3

Evidence Uncovered

Copyright © 2022 by Jacquelin Thomas

For questions and comments about the quality of this book, please contact us at CustomerService@Harlequin.com.

Love Inspired
22 Adelaide St. West, 41st Floor
Toronto, Ontario M5H 4E3, Canada
www.LoveInspired.com

Printed in U.S.A.

For I reckon that the sufferings of this present time are not worthy to be compared with the glory which shall be revealed in us.
—*Romans* 8:18

TERM KEY

MO—Modus Operandi

APB—All Points Bulletin

BOLO—Be On the Look Out

UNSUB—Unknown Subject

Chapter One

The November air caressed Lanier Barrow's skin as she got out of the rental car. Her heart racing, she stood on the sidewalk, staring at the corroded chain link fence that once surrounded the dilapidated house that had seen better days and currently lacked the love of a family. The weather-beaten porch leaned to the right side. From where she stood, Lanier had a perfect view of where pieces of the roof had been ripped away.

Amazingly, the house had survived the wrath of Hurricane Katrina in 2005, but another storm of that magnitude would most likely destroy what was left of it. A once-pink bicycle lay on its side, partially entangled in the debris of branches from an oak tree in the front yard. When she first drove into Kenner, Lanier noticed that the playground was approaching its pre-hurricane condition. Years later, New Orleans was still recovering and rebuilding.

On impulse, Lanier freed the rust-encrusted bicycle and parked it on the side of the house.

A cool fall breeze stole through the air, forcing her to pull the folds of her navy blazer together as a bone-deep chill washed over her. She swallowed the despair in her throat. It wasn't the weather prompting this reaction—it was returning to this house.

She glanced around, searching to see if anyone seemed particularly interested in a woman they'd never seen before checking out the abandoned house. There was only one person outside, an elderly lady two houses down, sitting in a swing on her porch. She sang as she rocked back and forth, not once glancing in Lanier's direction.

She opened the driver's side door and slid behind the wheel, skimmed the area once more, then started the car.

When Lanier pulled away from the curb, she peered in the rearview mirror to make sure she wasn't being followed.

I'm being paranoid, she told herself. *Nobody knows who I am.* And Lanier hoped to keep it that way.

If anyone decided to check her file, they would find that Special Agent Lanier Barrow had been an exceptional student, graduating high school at fifteen; she'd received her PhD in forensic psychology at twenty-two and begun working with the FBI immediately after graduation. Since joining the bureau four years ago, Lanier had successfully solved four overseas kidnapping cases and helped to end a religious zealot's siege.

The murders of three women over the course of three months now brought her to New Orleans. She believed their deaths were connected to a series of cold case files, and the reason Lanier asked specifically to be assigned to the interagency task force was the similarities in the way all the women died—strangulation.

Twenty years ago, the historic metropolis once dubbed the Land of Dreams by Louis Armstrong became a nightmare for the people of the Crescent City as the bodies of nearly two dozen women from Tremé turned up in outlying canals situated along highways bordering the western banks of Lake Pontchartrain.

An FBI task force was assigned to investigate the crimes back then, but they found no solid suspects; the investigation led to a dead end and eventually fell from the media spotlight as other murder cases took precedence over the older ones. The files were packed away and stored in the cold case file room.

The people of New Orleans and surrounding communities were able to breathe a sigh of relief when the killings came to a sudden halt. However, since August 13, three victims were recovered near the same area where the other women had been found.

Lanier hoped to find the person responsible before any other murders were committed.

The GPS directed her to the First District Police Department on Rampart Street, which covered the mid-city. After a brief meeting with the captain, Lanier was directed to Detective Daniel Jordan, the lead on the investigation. She was told that he and his partner, Michael Durousseau, were well-respected officers among members of law enforcement and the community. Jordan had been on call the night the first body was found the second week in August by a couple of teens playing hooky from school.

Switching her large designer tote from one shoulder to the other, Lanier found the detective in the break room at a table, eating lunch alone and reading a Bible.

Her initial assessment of Daniel showed that he was late twenties, maybe early thirties; clearly a man of faith and most likely a by-the-book detective, by his personage. He was what she could only describe as picture-perfect handsome. Jaw-dropping caramel-brown eyes and a neatly trimmed mustache accentuated the roasted chestnut hue of his complexion. He was dressed in a pair of black trousers, a cream-colored shirt and solid black tie, along with his badge, a pair of nickel handcuffs and a leather holster for his gun. His duty weapon was most likely locked in the top drawer of his desk, standard protocol in some stations.

Clearing her throat softly, Lanier addressed him. "Detective Jordan…"

He glanced up, looking her straight in the eye, his gaze unwavering. "That's me. What can I do for you?"

"I'm Special Agent Lanier Barrow with the FBI," she responded, taking the liberty of sitting down at his table without invitation. "I'm here at the request of your captain to offer my assistance with the investigation of the recent murders."

He looked as if he were weighing her words. After a moment, he asked, "Why is the FBI interested in these cases?"

"Because I'm ninety-nine point nine percent sure that the Crescent City Strangler is back." The serial killer was given the moniker by local media outlets twenty years ago when he held the city in a grip of fear. Lanier wasn't going to let this happen a second time.

Daniel's jaw dropped slightly as he tried not to stare. He was completely caught off guard by the woman sitting across from him. Special Agent Barrow was *stunning*, with expressive dark chocolate eyes, high cheekbones and complexion that was a mixture of honey and peanut butter. Her dark brown hair was pulled back into a neat bun at the nape of her neck.

She sat there without an ounce of irritation in her gaze as she patiently awaited his response.

He slowly released the breath he'd been holding. "I'm afraid I don't agree with your theory, Special Agent Barrow. I believe we have a new threat here in New Orleans."

"Please…call me Lanier, and I'll call you Daniel," she interjected with a smile. "There's no need to be so formal. We'll be working together." Leaning forward, hands clasped together, she asked, "I'm curious, though. What leads you to believe we're looking for a different unsub?"

Daniel displayed an outward calm, but he was riveted by her compelling eyes. Yet losing control over his emotions was not an option.

His focus needed to be on the job. The crime rate in New Orleans had been low for the past twenty years, and now women in his district were being stalked and killed. Finding the person responsible was a priority for him, as there was a lot of pressure from the mayor and the community. "These women were found near the same general area as the previous murders that took place years ago, but there's no connection," he said. "The vics back then were prostitutes and strippers, but the three women found recently—one was some type of data analyst, the other a secretary and the last a grocery store manager. The only common thread is that they were strangled."

"Serial killers have been known to alter and refine their MOs to accommodate new circumstances or skills," Lanier responded. "I know that the cold cases were all deemed to be sex crimes except for one. These latest victims weren't violated sexually. For some reason, he is targeting married women. The assailant took their wedding bands."

Their gazes locked as they appraised each other.

His partner, Michael, suddenly appeared in the doorway, announcing, "Hey, just got a call. They found another body. We gotta go."

Daniel released a long sigh of frustration. "That's the fourth one." He didn't like the way the body count was rising. He loved this city and vowed to protect New Orleans to the best of his ability, but right now, Daniel felt helpless. There wasn't any such thing as a perfect crime, he kept telling himself. The killer would make a mistake at some point, and they'd find him.

Another woman dead.

He walked briskly to his desk, dropped the Bible and grabbed his navy jacket with NOPD patches on each shoulder.

"I'm going to the crime scene with you," Lanier stated without preamble, cutting into his thoughts.

Daniel wasn't aware that she'd followed him out of the break room. His captain had briefed him on Lanier's achievements before her arrival. His initial impression of her was that she was passionate in her pursuit of the Crescent City Strangler. Perhaps to make a name for herself with the FBI. He didn't care what her motive was—he just wanted the murders to stop.

As if she could read his mind, Lanier said, "Look, I'm here to help make sure your district isn't left with another rash of *unsolved* cases like it was years ago. The task force in the past wasn't able to identify the perpetrator, but we've got modern technology on our side."

"She's right," his partner stated, then extended his hand. "I'm Michael Durousseau."

Looking him in the eye, Lanier accepted his firm handshake. "It's very nice to meet you."

"We're grateful for your assistance."

She slipped on her dark designer sunglasses. "I'll ride with y'all."

Daniel glanced over at his partner and shrugged. Agent Barrow had only arrived moments before, and she was all ready to dive right into the investigation. The woman was ambitious, but she had yet to realize they were looking for two different killers.

Chewing on a toothpick, Michael's face burst into a grin. "This is going to be interesting."

"C'mon…" Daniel muttered. There wasn't time to waste. They needed to get to the crime scene.

"A couple of froggers found the body," Michael stated during the drive. "She'd been discarded in a canal two miles from where our first victim was discovered."

When they arrived, Lanier was the first one out of the vehicle. Her eyes beheld the grim sight before her. Orange evidence cones were placed around a trash-strewn area and along the banks of the canal. Yellow tape roped off the scene to keep unauthorized persons from contaminating evidence. The body was covered with a white tarp. Crime scene technicians moved about in jackets emblazoned with the words New Orleans Police Crime Lab.

"I suggest we start with the body and work backward," she said, "which will hopefully help us narrow down our suspect pool."

"Because the body is the only constant in the murders…" Daniel glanced around the taped area. "All the victims were found along this same area, like the earlier crimes, but this doesn't mean it's the Crescent City Strangler. This perp is intentionally trying to mislead us." He didn't want to believe that Lanier's theory was correct. Twenty years had passed. Why would he suddenly start up again? Why now?

Techs covered the area, searching for evidence, photographing and bagging fragments of different items like cigarette butts and gum wrappers. One of the technicians poured a powdered stone material mixed with water into footprints and tire marks. When it dried, they would have a three-dimensional model of the impression.

Lanier slipped on a pair of purple plastic gloves, a contrast to the navy tailored slacks she wore with a matching blazer and a crisp, white button-down shirt underneath. She also wore a pair of low-heeled navy-blue leather pumps. Silver stud earrings and sheer tinted lip gloss completed her look. "Make sure to canvass the area thoroughly. This area just might offer certain clues about the unsub."

"We know the job," Michael stated. "We've done this more than a few times."

Ignoring his comment, she led the way to where the partially clothed corpse lay. Lanier pulled the sheet back and stared at the discoloration of the body. "What is the estimated time of death?" she asked the coroner.

"Between sixty and seventy-two hours ago."

"Can you tell if the body was violated in any way?"

"No. I'll know more after the autopsy."

She leaned in closer. "I need a pair of tweezers or small tongs."

Lanier signaled for a tech to join her. "There's something in her hair. It could be fiber from a rope or rug."

The CSI technician collected the fiber with tweezers

and placed it in a clear tube, then labeled and placed it inside a carrier with the other evidence.

She pointed to the victim's neck. "There's a lot of bruising on her hands and neck, which means she most likely put up a fight before or while she was being strangled."

The coroner agreed. "Her larynx was crushed like the other three."

Lanier glanced up at Daniel. His eyes were closed, and his expression was one of profound sadness. Just in the short time she'd talked with him, she knew each victim meant something to Daniel. Although they disagreed when it came to the unsub, the one thing they had in common was that they both wanted justice for the victims and their families.

As Daniel always did whenever there was a victim, dead or alive, he whispered a silent prayer for them.

When he was done, Daniel studied the corpse.

"I can't believe Captain West brought the FBI in on this," Michael said in a low voice. It makes us look incompetent…like we can't solve our own cases."

"It's not that," Daniel responded. "The FBI sent Lanier because they believe the Crescent City Strangler is back and that he's responsible for these new vics. They want to finally close all those cold cases."

Michael looked surprised. "Really? Our vics aren't strippers or prostitutes. In fact, they have all been married women. I know one was going through a divorce, and another recently separated. I agree we have a serial killer on our hands, but it's not the Crescent City Strangler. Just doesn't feel right to me."

"I agree, but it seems Lanier and the bureau are convinced otherwise," Daniel responded, briefly considering Lanier's theory that all four deaths were possibly linked to the Crescent City Strangler. If there was the slightest possibility, he had to know for sure. The last thing Daniel wanted was for his beloved city to once again be gripped by fear. "As far as I'm concerned, it really doesn't matter. I want whoever is responsible off the streets before any more women go missing."

Michael nodded. "If they're right, then we can definitely use the help."

Daniel's eyes landed briefly on Lanier just as she moved the tote from her right to her left shoulder. He observed as she interacted with members of the CSI team. She was professional, asking questions without a hint of arrogance or rudeness. Lanier appeared to be unaware of the captivating picture she made whenever she smiled. Something intense flared through his entrancement, which was disturbing to Daniel in every way.

She glanced over in his direction.

He exchanged a nod with Lanier, then turned his attention to the young police officer who suddenly appeared by his side. She carried a packet, which she presented to him.

He quickly signed and accepted the information on another case he had been working on. He walked it over to the detective that would be taking over that particular case.

Daniel wanted to give the recent string of victims his full attention.

Chapter Two

Lanier trod carefully through the crime scene area a second time, searching for additional evidence to be sent to the investigative and forensic teams back at the bureau. She examined the surrounding area slowly, taking in every detail, committing them to memory.

"Whoever did this is very organized," Daniel stated when he joined her.

"I agree," she responded. "He's impulsive, but he's also methodical in planning his crimes. He kills them in one place and disposes of them here. He could drop the bodies in a swamp where the alligators could eat off them, but instead he places them where they can be found. He *wants* us to find them. This isn't the work of an amateur, Daniel. He's had enough experience to maintain a high degree of control over the crime scene. He's been doing this a long time."

"He *wants* to make it look like the Crescent City Strangler has suddenly reappeared. I'm telling you that this isn't the same person who did the killings twenty years ago." Daniel walked over to a pile of dirt and bent down, eyeballing it closer. "I do agree with you that he wants us to discover the bodies. I'll wager he's following the investigation closely in the news media and wanting the attention."

"He could be attention-seeking," Lanier stated, "but I don't get that feeling. This is more about his arrogance and the *message*."

"So you think the killer we're looking for is trying to send a message?" Michael inquired. "It's my understanding the most serial killers want the world to recognize them for their work."

"My instincts tell me that this goes a bit deeper than that," Lanier stated. "The killer isn't looking for recognition. He's sending a message. We need to find out what that message is—get into his head."

"With the Crescent City Strangler, he had a hatred of strippers and prostitutes. The person we're looking for now... I agree with Michael. He wants recognition," Daniel said. "Because he has his own signature. He wants the world to remember him and his work."

Lanier held back her irritation with the handsome detective. "Right now, we have a difference of opinion, but I'm going to prove to the two of you that the person we're looking for is the same one who killed all those women twenty years ago." Her tone brooked no argument, and she glanced back at the crime scene. "I guess we're done here."

They walked to the car in silence, and Michael joined them a moment later.

Once they were on the road, she said, "I have to check in to the hotel, then get on a conference call with my team. If you two don't have plans for later this evening, why don't y'all meet me for dinner? It's on me. We can continue our discussion on the current *and* cold case Crescent City Strangler files. Hopefully a nice meal will warm you and Michael to the long hours of work ahead of us." They needed to be of one mind, and Lanier knew it was going to take some solid evidence to convince Daniel and his partner that they were looking for the same unsub.

"As much as I hate to turn down a free meal, I'm afraid I won't be able to make dinner," Michael said. "I have to attend my daughter's school recital. You and Daniel gon' be on your own tonight. No babysitter this evening."

Daniel gave her a polite smile. "Looks like it'll just be the two of us."

"You pick the restaurant," Lanier stated. "I want the best seafood New Orleans has to offer."

"I know just the place. Ellie's Seafood in the French Quarter is where you want to eat."

Michael echoed Daniel's sentiment. "I hate that I'm gon' miss it. I love that restaurant, but daddy duty calls."

"How many children do you have?" Lanier asked, turning in her seat to face him. Michael had graciously allowed her to sit in the front seat with Daniel.

"Two," he responded. "A son and a daughter. You have any?"

She shook her head no. "I'm way too busy—no time to even think about a family." The truth was that she avoided relationships because she was afraid of losing another person she loved. It was better to keep a wall erected around her heart. She chose to focus on her career, but not for advancement. From the moment she'd studied the case in college, it had always been her desire to put the Crescent City Strangler behind bars for life.

* * *

Seated at his desk, Daniel found himself looking forward to sharing a meal with the beautiful FBI agent. He was curious to learn more about her. He preferred getting to know a person he had to work closely with—it helped if their personalities meshed well, as Daniel didn't like conflict. But first, he had to quell the odd fluttering within him when she was close. He cautioned himself against thinking of Lanier in a romantic way. He didn't want distractions of any kind.

Michael intruded on his thoughts by saying, "Agent Barrow seems nice enough. A little bossy, but she's definitely easy on the eyes."

Daniel nodded perfunctorily. "Lanier's beautiful, certainly smarter than you and me… She finished high school at fifteen and grad school at twenty-two. She's the type of woman who goes after what she wants."

"I see you read her file. She's no different than you or me—we all have the same goal. We want to find this killer." Michael's eyebrows arched mischievously. He sat back, rubbing his bald head. "Should be an interesting dinner tonight."

"You're sure that you can't make it?"

"Surely you're not afraid to be alone with Agent Barrow," Michael responded with a short laugh.

"Naw, I'm not. If you were there, it'd save me from having to relay everything we talk about to you later."

Michael turned up his smile a notch. "Hey, I'm your partner."

"You're nosy," Daniel stated, his mouth quirked with humor. He and Michael had been partners for eight years now. He had a lot of respect for the single father and considered him a friend.

"A quality that makes me a good detective," he responded.

The telephone on Michael's desk rang.

Releasing a short sigh, he answered it. "Detective Durousseau speaking..."

Daniel turned his attention to a manila file on his desk. It was a witness statement from a fatal shooting that had taken place a week ago. He decided to hand it off to another detective so he could focus on the murdered women.

The day passed quickly because of the amount of paperwork on his desk and having spent most of the morning at the crime site. He didn't mind, though. Daniel liked keeping busy, but he didn't like people dying. He worked homicide because he wanted to protect and serve. He wanted to uncover the truth for a victim's loved ones and bring criminals to justice.

Before leaving the station, he stopped to update his supervisor on a couple of pending cases that would also be handled by some of the other detectives.

Daniel checked his watch, then strode quickly to his car. He was meeting Lanier in an hour. The prolonged anticipation was almost unbearable, but he dismissed the feeling as nothing more than a fleeting one. Daniel couldn't allow his emotions to overrule his brain, taking the focus off his work. He'd made that mistake once before—he wouldn't do it again.

The first time nearly cost him his life.

Lanier paced across the floor of the living area in her suite.

Why did I invite this man to dinner?

She figured a meal together would lay a firm foundation on which to work together. For the interagency task force to be successful, they would have to trust one another and work as a team.

Lanier changed into a black-and-white pinstripe jacket, a red blouse and black jeans. She decided to pull her hair into a ponytail. Her look was comfortable, but still professional. This was a business dinner, not a date.

She sat down on the edge of the king-sized bed in the well-appointed room with upscale amenities. Lanier had chosen a hotel situated at the crossroads of Royal and Canal Streets in the French Quarter at the suggestion of her aunt June who grew up in New Orleans. It served as the perfect home away from home. Outside she could hear the bustling sounds of the red streetcars with gold trim down below going back and forth.

The restaurant was located on the corner of Canal and Bourbon, a short distance from the hotel, so she didn't have far to go. Lanier examined her reflection in the mirror. Satisfied with her look, she picked up the car keys and left the suite.

Ten minutes later, she walked across the parking lot toward the entrance of Ellie's Seafood. Lanier paused to take a cleansing breath before going inside. She had no problem being a team player and hoped the same of Daniel. During the meal, her goal was to find some common ground in their different theories regarding the unsub and convince him to keep an open mind.

Daniel was already inside waiting for her when she opened the door. His steady gaze bore into Lanier, causing her pulse to pound. His caramel eyes and neat mustache complemented his handsome face. Earlier at the crime scene, he'd seemed to have the ability to put those around him at ease almost immediately.

"You have any trouble getting here?" he asked.

"Not at all," she responded. "My hotel is on Canal and Royal."

A delectable aroma drifted from the kitchen, greeting Daniel and Lanier. She noticed the dining room was filled with a nice crowd of people enjoying their evening meals. The clinking of glasses and dishes and the sound of laughter was like music to her ears.

"I have to warn you," Daniel said. "They give you large servings here."

Lanier grinned. "Doesn't scare me."

They were seated a few minutes later at a table in a traditional Vieux Carré courtyard, surrounded by lush native tropical plants, fountains and brick pavers. Lanier settled back in her chair, looking around, taking in the ambiance and the view. "This is a nice place."

"Wait until you try the food," Daniel said.

She noticed he was watching her intently. She shifted in her chair, ignoring the tingling in the pit of her stomach, but Lanier welcomed the surge of excitement she felt at the opportunity to work alongside Daniel on the investigation. She didn't get the impression he had a huge ego or that he had to be right all the time. Lanier couldn't stand working with people like that—it was hard to accomplish much when interagency task forces consisted of personalities that didn't mesh well.

We'll make a good team. There wasn't a hint of arrogance about Daniel, and he'd listened to her theory despite believing otherwise.

"You look deep in thought."

She glanced over at Daniel. "Sorry. My mind drifted to the investigation and what needs to be done. The first thing I need to do is review all the cold case files related to the Crescent City Strangler."

"There are twenty-four cases," Daniel said. "And those are only the ones we know about."

"Tomorrow I'll get started with the first six victims."

He took a sip of his water. "I'll make sure you get them."

Lanier's skin warmed under his scrutiny. Daniel was openly studying her as if trying to read her thoughts. "If you're wondering whether I came here just to make a name for myself, you're wrong," Lanier stated. "I want the same thing you do."

"Justice…"

"Yes," she responded. "Now that we've gotten that out of the way, I need to figure out what to order."

Lanier could tell Daniel wasn't sure what to make of her.

She preferred it this way.

"Why are you convinced this is the work of the Crescent City Strangler?" Daniel asked, picking up the menu. "And if it is—why do you suppose he's suddenly resurfaced now?" He found himself intrigued by Lanier's theory. Twenty years ago, an FBI task force assigned to investigate the Crescent City Strangler had suggested that two unsubs were responsible for the deaths. But this latest wave of killings was very clearly the work of one person—Daniel believed they had a copycat on their hands.

"He could've just gotten out of prison for another crime," Lanier offered as she scanned the enticing offerings. "Maybe he recently moved back to New Orleans, or there was simply a cooling-off period. This unsub could most likely be triggered by problems with finances, employment, family or marital issues. Maybe that's why he's targeting married women."

He considered her response, then said, "Some of the earlier victims were strangled by hand. He then started using rope. My victims were strangled with rope, but a different technique was used."

"The unsub used a double coil of rope in the past, but now he's fashioned it into a handmade garrote—a method used in the seventeenth or eighteenth century," Lanier stated. "The bodies that landed on your desk all had their larynx crushed. That's because the unsub places a knot at the center. He applies additional pressure by placing his knee or foot in the victim's back. He's angry and wants to punish these women."

Daniel was trying to keep an open mind, but this just didn't add up to him. It seemed like too many shifts. It had to be a different person. "The Crescent City Strangler never changed his MO."

"The last known victim twenty years ago wasn't a prostitute or stripper," Lanier stated. "Gayle Giraud. She was a student who worked part-time as a bartender."

"We don't know this for sure," Daniel argued. "Maybe she needed to make a little extra money on the side."

She swallowed as if uncomfortable. "There's nothing to suggest Gayle was anything other than a bartender and a student nurse," Lanier insisted. "For whatever reason, killing her must have done something to the unsub. Maybe he felt guilty over his mistake and stopped."

Daniel took a sip of the chilled water in his glass, then returned it gently to the table. He shifted slightly in his seat and said, "The last time someone from the bureau helped, they couldn't find anything solid."

"I studied these cases in grad school and in training for the bureau, Daniel. The FBI's profile of the unsub describes him as being charming, intelligent and living a normal life. He could be your neighbor, your best friend or even a family member. When you look at all the victims, they are all around the same age and physical appearance and have spent quite a bit of time in bars or worked the streets. The recent victims are women with conventional jobs who enjoyed going out on the weekends to bars and clubs."

Daniel still couldn't reconcile that all the killings were the work of one person. "Lanier, I think we have to at least consider the possibility that we may have a copycat on our hands."

"That's plausible," she responded. "We'll know for sure when the lab work comes back. Rope fibers were found on one of the women twenty years ago. There was some on the most recent victim. If the rope comes back a match, we'll have a strong reason to connect these cases to the Crescent City Strangler."

He listened in bewilderment. "That's kind of a long stretch, don't you think? The chances of the rope matching are slim to none."

Seemingly unbothered by his words, Lanier smiled. "Shall we order?"

Daniel knew they had to check out every available avenue to find the killer, but he felt she was wrong. Why would a person who'd managed to evade capture all these years suddenly come out of retirement?

When the server came to take their order, Lanier chose the crab quartet, which consisted of four crab dishes on one plate—crabmeat au gratin, crab balls, fried softshell crab and fried crab claws—while Daniel decided on the crawfish étouffée.

He was surprised when Lanier ordered a bowl of gumbo to go.

"I'll have it for dinner tomorrow," she explained. "I don't really enjoy eating alone in restaurants." Lanier's smile was like a ray of sunshine, stretching out to wrench him from behind the wall Daniel hadn't even realized he'd been hiding behind.

"I almost prefer it," Daniel said. "I don't eat out much, though. I enjoy cooking, so I make my meals and have the leftovers for lunch." His gaze traveled to Lanier. "Do you cook?"

"Yes, but I travel quite a bit, so I'm forced to eat out."

"I know you're not fond of dining alone, but do you enjoy traveling?" He was careful to keep his tone and questions professional, although he wanted to learn so much more about the beautiful woman sitting across from him. Daniel's attraction was disturbing to him. It conflicted with his policy of not dating coworkers, even temporary members of his team. Daniel had been involved with another officer once, and during a shoot-out, he couldn't focus clearly because she'd placed herself in the line of fire. His first thought had been to protect her. He was shot and nearly died during that incident. After that, Daniel decided to keep his personal and professional life separate.

"I do, but I have to admit there are times when I get tired of living out of a suitcase."

Her response was a solid reminder that once the killer was apprehended, Lanier would be leaving. Daniel wasn't looking forward to when that time came.

Chapter Three

A few hours later, Lanier and Daniel left the parking lot, driving in opposite directions from the restaurant.

Although most of their discussion was about the investigation, she'd gotten several glimpses into Daniel's quiet nature, sharp mind and subtle humor.

There were moments when Lanier wondered if, like her, Daniel was haunted by something that had driven him into this line of work. Or was he an adrenaline junkie who simply got high off danger? In her line of work, she saw them all the time—men and women who lived for the thrill of the adventure and thought nothing of placing their lives in danger. It wasn't a quality she found attractive.

It was still too early to tell exactly what type of man he was, but she trusted her instincts. She thought about the Bible he kept at his desk and wondered how he balanced his faith with being a homicide detective. *Maybe one day I'll ask him.* She couldn't fathom how he could believe in a loving God with so much evil in the world. In his line of work, Daniel confronted it daily. Yet he didn't appear jaded. Instead, it seemed like a light glimmered over his face like beams of reflected radiance.

She drove into the hotel parking lot, turned off the ignition and got out.

Lanier was about to walk toward the hotel entrance when the hairs on the back of her neck stood to attention and her heartbeat began racing. Her hearing was very sensitive. She glanced around, one hand on her gun, her eyes searching for movement. Lanier became increasingly uneasy. A warning voice whispered in her head. Someone was watching her—she could almost feel their angry gaze on her.

The sound of a vehicle door closing captured her attention. She spotted a lone man around mid-forties, dressed in a pair of jeans and a denim shirt, walking to the front entrance of the hotel.

He never once looked her way.

She bit her bottom lip and forced her body to relax. Her watcher was still out there somewhere, hidden in the shadows, his body merged into the ominous silhouettes of the buildings dotted along the street. Lanier knew he wanted her to know he was there. Her fear gave him power.

I'm not afraid of you, was the message she wanted to send with her body language. Her eyes darting around her as she walked, Lanier removed her hand from the holstered gun. She reached inside her purse, retrieved her key card, and navigated toward the entrance of the hotel.

Her ever observant gaze was trained on the reflective glass across the front of the building. If there was movement of any kind, she'd notice.

As soon as Lanier was safely inside her suite, she took

a deep breath to calm the adrenaline racing through her body and quiet her thoughts.

Hand on her gun, she made sure the room was secure before locking the door, then removed her jacket and placed her holster and gun on the nightstand next to the king-sized bed.

Lanier put her gumbo in the mini-fridge, inserted a chamomile and honey herbal tea K-Cup into the Keurig, then jumped into the shower.

Afterward, dressed in a tank top and pajama pants, Lanier grabbed her tea and settled down on the sofa, focusing her thoughts on the stack of files she'd brought home with her. She went back over the notes concerning the recent victims.

Every now and then, Lanier would reach for the cup that rested on the table and took a sip of the liquid. Its warmth soothed and relaxed her. Lanier loved her job, but the worst part of it was having to travel thirty percent of the time, missing out on precious family time with her aunt and uncle, who'd adopted her when she was six years old. When she wasn't on the road, Lanier spent most weekends working to stay on top of her cases and teaching self-defense classes, which didn't leave much time for a social life. However, she made a point to make it to Sunday dinners with her family and girls' nights out with her best friend, Celine, twice a month.

A second cup of tea later, she sat cross-legged in the middle of the king-sized bed, reviewing the photos of the recent victims, reports and evidence documentation. It was past midnight.

Lanier turned off her laptop and wondered if the person watching her earlier was still out there. She thought about going back downstairs to do some surveillance of her own but decided against it. If someone was truly after her, they would come for her in the suite—and she would be ready.

The next day, Lanier was provided a temporary office at the station. Inside, the dove-gray walls were sparse, without artwork. A forty-inch television was mounted on the wall facing her desk. There was one window to the outside. In the middle of the room was a bare desk made of dark wood and a leather chair. Beside the desk sat a stack of six boxes with names and dates on them.

"Good morning," Daniel greeted her. He carried a medium-sized white box over to her desk and set it down. "I see someone already placed the cold case files in here."

Lanier smiled at him. "Captain West was gracious enough to let me use this room while I'm here." Pointing to the box he was holding, she asked, "What's all this?"

"Just a few supplies I thought you'd need while you're working here. Pens, Post-it notes, legal pads, highlighters…office stuff."

She was touched by his thoughtfulness. "Thanks. Who do I see about a really large whiteboard? I need one for this wall."

"I'll put in a request for it."

Michael paused in her doorway long enough to hold up his hand in greeting, then said, "I'm headed to the break room. You need anything? I'm no good until I've had at least two cups of coffee."

"I'm fine," Lanier responded, "but thank you, Michael."

Daniel asked, "Can you think of anything else you might need?"

Lanier pointed to the boxes of cold case files for the first six victims of the Crescent City Strangler on the floor. "I'm good for right now."

"Michael and I have to talk to some people regarding another case. I'll be out for a couple of hours."

"Okay," she responded. "I'll see you when you get back."

Lanier watched the two men leave. Their body language and occasional light banter indicated that they weren't just partners. They were also friends. Daniel appeared more reserved while Michael seemed outgoing. They balanced each other out.

She stole a peek at the clock.

I need to get to work.

Lanier spent the entire day going through box after box of cold case files, auditing the documentation, evidence and crime scene photos. She jotted down her own notes as she reviewed each case.

Lanier examined each crime scene photo carefully, hoping for something to jump out at her. The unsub was goal-oriented, but he killed in one location and disposed of the bodies in another. This was rare for this type of serial killer—a goal-oriented one.

Reviewing the notes, Lanier sighed in frustration. No one had been able to find any evidence offering clues as to the location where the victims were murdered. Only two so far appeared to have been killed outdoors, suggested by the evidence found on their clothing.

She pushed away from the desk and rose to her feet, then ventured into the break room to make a cup of herbal tea. And minutes later, she returned to the office and the stack of files waiting on her desk. Humming softly, Lanier sat down and went back to reviewing more case files.

Daniel and Michael returned.

"You're back much sooner than I thought you'd be," she said when Daniel ventured into her office.

"We talked to the perp's mother, but she either didn't know anything or she was a good liar. The same thing with his brother, but luckily his sister had much more to say."

Lanier leaned back in her chair. "What happened?"

"A young woman, Mary Adams, was shot in the parking lot of the store where she was employed. She was separated from her husband and was the mother of a six-month-old."

"You suspect the husband?"

"He looks good for it. He's abusive and once threatened to kill her if she ever tried to leave him," Daniel said in a dull and troubled voice. "She left him a month ago, and now she's dead. His own sister helped Mary leave."

"Does he have an alibi?"

"Not a strong one," he replied, his fists clenched tight and nostrils flaring. "We're hoping we can locate some video of what happened."

"Daniel, you look frustrated."

"*I am.* A mother is dead. A little boy will have to grow up without his mother possibly because of his father. If he is responsible for her death, I want that murderer off the streets. I can't help but wonder if he'll ever have the courage to look his son in the eye."

A vein in his neck pulsed. Daniel released a slow breath.

"I detest domestic violence," Lanier stated. "It's why

I was teaching self-defense classes to women before I came here. There's power in being able to fight back."

Daniel eyed her. "Sounds like you know this from experience."

"I've never been abused by anyone, but I know how it feels to be helpless and powerless," Lanier said. "I will never allow myself to be someone's victim—not without a fight."

Daniel glanced at his watch. It was almost three o'clock, and he hadn't touched his lunch.

They had all been so caught up with the investigations of the latest victims, none of them realized how much time passed. "My stomach's growling, so I'm going to take a short break to eat something," he said.

Lanier glanced up from the file she was reading. "I didn't realize it was this late. I'll run across the street and grab a salad. I can eat while I work."

"Take a real break," Daniel said. "Join me for lunch." Holding up a folder, he added, "We can all use a mental break from this stuff." He could tell Lanier was as hyper-focused as he was when it came to investigating a case. She'd only taken a couple of bathroom breaks throughout the day thus far.

"We all need to eat something," Michael responded. "Lanier, I'll walk over with you. I'm starving."

"I'm ready." She pushed away from the desk and stretched. "Daniel, do you want anything?"

"I brought my lunch, but thanks."

Michael rose to his feet and followed her out of the office.

Daniel caught the way his partner was eyeing Lanier and felt a thin thread of jealousy. He quickly forced the notion out of his mind. He had no right to these feelings. If he kept a professional distance from her, they just might be able to stay alive during the hunt for a murderer.

Chapter Four

Lanier's stomach growled in protest. She had a habit of skipping lunch whenever she was consumed with an investigation. Her aunt, a nutritionist, suggested she set a reminder on her phone to make sure she ate at least three meals a day. Lanier had yet to do it.

"Have you been to New Orleans before now? If not, you are in for a thrill," Michael said as they walked across the tiled floor toward the exit doors.

Her face brightened at his question. "That's what I keep hearing. Hopefully, I'll have some time to explore the Big Easy before I have to go back home to Virginia."

"You should take a day or two off. There's a lot to see and do here."

"Maybe after we find the unsub."

They crossed the street and entered the deli. Lanier scanned the menu while Michael ordered a shrimp po'boy sandwich dressed. When it was her turn, she ordered the Cobb salad with blackened chicken and honey mustard dressing. They continued to make small talk while waiting on their food.

Daniel was already seated at a table in the break room

when they returned. He moved his Bible to make room for her while Michael sat opposite him. He reached into a lunch bag and pulled out a sandwich.

"We aren't interrupting your study, are we?" Lanier asked.

"I read while y'all were out," Daniel responded. "I'm good."

"You're dedicated for sure." She placed a napkin in her lap. "I haven't read mine in a long time."

"My Bible is still in the packaging it came in," Michael interjected, then popped a shred of lettuce hanging from his sandwich into his mouth.

Shaking his head, Daniel uttered, "I gave you that a couple of years ago."

He shrugged. "I know, and I appreciate the gift, but man... I read enough here at work. Reading was never my thing."

"That's sad, because there's a library named after your family at the university," Daniel stated.

Michael gave a small chuckle. "It's ironic."

Lanier sliced off a piece of chicken and stuck it in her mouth, chewing slowly. "You're related to *that* Durousseau family?"

"Yep—by adoption, anyway. My birth mother is white, and her family didn't want a black grandchild. After Iris Durousseau had several miscarriages, she and her husband, Robert, decided to consider adoption because he wanted an heir. They adopted me when I was two years old."

"I read an article about them some years ago." Lanier didn't mention that it was about them being the wealthiest family in New Orleans. Robert Durousseau was a descendent of the first families who came from France.

Daniel glanced at her, then said, "We're talking about ourselves. I apologize for being rude."

"Oh no..." she responded. "I'm enjoying the conversation. How long have you worked together? Because you sound like a married couple."

"About eight years now," Daniel responded. "He's been my partner since I started as a rookie."

"My last partner left the agency for a position with Homeland Security," she said. "I'll have a new one when I get back to Virginia."

They fell into silence as they continued to eat their meals. "The unsub has definitely wrapped this city in fear," Lanier said as casually as she could manage. She wiped her mouth with her napkin, then took a sip of bottled water. She'd debated whether to tell them about the incident the night before.

"Why do you say that?" Daniel asked. He looked as if he were weighing her words.

"I'm pretty sure someone was watching me when I returned to the hotel last night. I felt it the moment I got out my car. There's a part of me that feels like it might have been the unsub."

"Did you see anybody?" Michael asked.

"No, I was very vigilant. I couldn't find him, but I knew he was there. I could *feel* him."

"You didn't notice anyone following you when you left the restaurant?" Daniel inquired.

Lanier shook her head. "I didn't. It's possible he was already at the hotel by the time I arrived. He could've followed me from the station earlier and was just sitting and waiting for me to return."

"But who would know that you're here or why?" Michael asked.

"I could've been seen at the crime scene. I'm an outsider. If it was the unsub, he probably gets some type of satisfaction in what he considers a game. His motivation for the killings can be intrinsic and may not ever be fully identified," Lanier stated. "If it's not the unsub, then it could be a reluctant witness, I guess."

"If it is the killer, do you think he could be targeting you as his next victim?" Michael asked.

Lanier finished off the last of her salad. "I hope so because I'm ready. I don't mind being the bait," she said without flinching, then pivoted. "Michael, how was the recital last night? How old are your children?" Lanier asked, trying to shift the subject, and shut off any further awareness of Daniel.

"Six and four," he responded.

"Those are great ages. I'm sure they're very curious about the world."

Michael smiled blandly, then finished up his sandwich and downed the last of his drink. "Time for me to get back to work." He stood up and left rather abruptly.

"Did I say something wrong?" she asked when he stalked out of the break room. She found his reaction to her comment strange, as if his mood shifted suddenly from light to dark.

"You have no way of knowing this, but Michael's wife walked out on him and the kids six months ago."

She shuddered in embarrassment. "Oh wow... I didn't know he was a single parent," Lanier said. "I really put my foot in my mouth this time. No wonder he looked so uncomfortable."

"Michael doesn't like to talk about it," Daniel stated, "but I know he was devastated. Carly was the love of his life."

"I feel so terrible for him. Being a single father and a police detective—it can't be easy."

Daniel rose to his feet. "You should know that your assessment was right. He loved being married, and Michael is devoted to his children."

She threw away her food container, wiped down the table with her napkin and walked back to her office while Daniel retrieved some files off his desk to return to the records department.

Minutes later, Michael knocked on her door. "Hey, I want to apologize for my reaction earlier. I didn't mean to be rude."

She glimpsed the pain that flickered in his eyes and felt empathy for him. "You don't owe me anything," Lanier responded. "I was trying to make conversation, but I never should've inquired about your private life."

"Daniel probably told you that my wife left me." Michael shook his head regretfully. "I'm still trying to process everything."

"I completely understand."

The silence between them thickened the air.

Clearing her throat, Lanier said, "No apology is necessary, but I appreciate it."

He smiled. "I'll let you get back to work."

Later that day, when Michael left to pick up his children from school, Daniel caught up with her in the copy room. "I saw Michael talking to you earlier. Everything okay?"

Lanier picked up the documents she'd made copies of, returning them to a folder. "He apologized to me when he didn't have to do so. It was a sweet gesture."

"He's a good man."

She glanced at the clock on the wall and said, "I think I'm going to leave a bit early today. I don't know about you, but I'm tired."

"I'll try to finish going through the videos from Celia's Bar. The very first victim, Monique Vega, met up with a couple of friends there. She disappeared on Friday the Thirteenth."

"I'd like to view it, too," Lanier stated, following him to his desk.

"She appears very flirtatious," she noted, staring at the computer monitor. "The killer could've targeted her because of it."

Pointing, Daniel said, "She's leaving the club alone. Here you see her talking to some guy in a car. Then she goes to her own vehicle and drives off. The vic looks to be heading home on the street cams, but there's no evidence she ever made it there."

She pulled up a chair beside him and sat down. "What about the guy that she stopped to talk to?"

"He went inside the club and stayed there until closing," Daniel responded.

"Did anyone else go to the house?"

"According to her husband, nothing was disturbed, which could mean that she may have been grabbed outside the house. Nothing stood out," Daniel said.

"This unsub has had years to perfect his technique. We can only hope he'll make a mistake at some point." Lanier chewed on her bottom lip as she considered several possible scenarios in her mind.

The Crescent City Strangler investigation had proven challenging to the investigating officers twenty years ago. But she was determined not to let the trail go cold once again with their current investigation.

* * *

Daniel leaned closer to Lanier for a better view of the monitor. Her body heat enveloped him and made him slightly dazed.

His attraction to her was not surprising. Daniel was drawn to her because they had been thrown together to work closely on this investigation. It would prove hard, but he didn't want to risk becoming distracted. Until they found the person responsible for the deaths of the four women, Daniel had to put up a wall around his emotions.

He opened another video file on screen. "This is the second victim. Just like Monique, it looks like she flirted and danced with a couple of different guys, but left the club alone," he said. "However, Carolyn Mays never made it to her car. There were no cameras in the back where she was parked."

"It's like she just disappeared into thin air," Lanier murmured. "It wouldn't matter if there were cameras. This unsub is very careful—he makes sure he's never seen on any camera." She sighed in annoyance.

Daniel could sense her frustration. He felt the same way.

"I wonder if we're seeing a trend. Maybe the unsub is somehow triggered by the women's flirtatious behavior."

"Could be, but it seems innocent enough," Daniel stated.

"Maybe not in the mind of the unsub," she responded. "He might feel these women deserve to be punished for their behavior."

An hour later, Lanier went to her office, picked up her tote and stopped at his desk long enough to say, "I'm going to the hotel. Just call me if something comes up."

"Hold up," he blurted. "I'll follow you there."

Looking at him, she said, "You really don't have to tail me to the hotel." Lanier didn't want to become a burden to Daniel, nor did she need saving. "I can handle myself."

"It's not negotiable," he responded. "I'm not gonna let you put your life in danger on my watch. Plus, if our killer is watching you—we may be able to catch him."

After making sure her suite was secure and getting settled, Lanier placed a quick call to check in with her aunt.

She ate the gumbo, showered, then dressed in a pair of shorts and tank top. She spent the next two hours going through a personal photo album, but the conversation with her aunt was still fresh in her mind hours later.

"Honey, your uncle and I are worried about you," her aunt had said. *"We just don't think it was a good idea for you to go back to New Orleans."*

"There's no need to worry," she'd tried to assure her. *"I'm being very careful. This is my job, Aunt June. All these women deserve justice, and we want to find the person responsible."*

"I agree, but it's been twenty years..."

"I'm not giving up, Auntie. Especially since four more women have since been murdered."

"Please be careful."

"I am."

"I love you, Lanier."

She'd broken into a sad smile. *"I love you, too."*

A photograph brought her attention back to the present. It was of her mother.

"I miss you so much, Mama," she whispered as she

allowed her grief to wash all over her. Her eyes filled with tears.

Lanier clenched her hand into a fist. "I promise I won't let the Crescent City Strangler get away this time. I'm going to find the person responsible for turning my world upside down when I was only six years old." She'd used the anger toward losing her mother to motivate her—to keep her focused on this one goal.

Gayle Giraud had attended nursing school during the day and worked as a bartender in the evenings, while Gayle's mother watched Lanier. The memory of the police showing up at her grandmother's house to deliver the news of Gayle's death was still very vivid in Lanier's mind.

"No, it's not her. This can't be true!" her grandmother had screamed hysterically.

Seeing her mother in a coffin at the funeral home was the most horrible thing Lanier had ever experienced in her entire life. She remembered pleading with her mother to wake up.

Six months later, Lanier's young heart broke once more when her grandmother, Estelle, passed away unexpectedly. This time she had to live in Richmond with her mom's sister, June, and husband, Allen Barrow.

Even now, she missed the life she would've had with her mother. Holidays, Mother's Day, her high school and college graduations—all her accomplishments—her mother wasn't there to celebrate with Lanier.

And so her mother's murder had ignited a hunger in her.

A hunger for revenge.

Chapter Five

Instead of leaving, Daniel found a dark, remote area to park, which provided him a clear view of the hotel entrance and parking lot. His eyes slowly surveyed the surroundings.

Nothing seemed out of place. It just looked like a normal night in New Orleans.

It was midweek, and there were a few guests checking in—nothing remarkable about any of them. A man dressed in a polo shirt, shorts, mid-calf socks and a pair of sandals. Accompanying him was a young woman Daniel knew was a call girl. He'd recalled seeing her a couple of times at the station.

Fifteen minutes later, a car pulled up, and an older couple got out and went inside. Two more couples checked in after that.

While he watched, Daniel listened to the audio version of scriptures from the book of James. He enjoyed reading the Bible or listening to it because it was here that he found his peace. It was in God's word that he found encouragement and hope. While listening, he continued searching for anything that appeared out of place.

There wasn't much point in his being there conducting surveillance because of the way the hotel was built—he had no idea which rooms guests entered or exited. He didn't even know Lanier's room number.

Daniel considered going into the lobby to sit, but he didn't want whoever was tailing the FBI agent to know he was there.

I'll already be here if she needs me.

A man still sitting in his car, talking on the phone, caught Daniel's attention. He'd noticed him earlier when Lanier first entered the hotel. Daniel captured a photograph of the vehicle and the man.

Ten minutes later, the guy drove off, enabling him to get a photo of the license plate.

The next couple of hours turned out to be uneventful.

Daniel didn't have to wonder what Lanier was doing right now. He was pretty sure she was in her room reviewing case files. She didn't know when to turn off. He recognized this quality in her because he possessed it as well.

A smile tugged at his lips as an image of Lanier formed in his mind. He admired her feisty and take-charge nature. Daniel had no doubt she could handle herself, but she wasn't invincible. He had always been drawn to strong women.

This time was no different.

The next day, Lanier noticed the dark circles beneath Daniel's eyes and the slight creases in his shirt, which were visible beneath his jacket, when he arrived for work. It looked like he'd just pulled the button-down out of its packaging.

He must have sat outside the hotel most of the night.

She was touched by this act of protectiveness. It was kind of nice having someone look out for her. She wouldn't admit this to Daniel, however.

Lanier brought him a cup of coffee. "I'm guessing you spent your evening doing surveillance?"

He nodded and offered a tired smile.

"I appreciate the gesture, but I told you I can take care of myself. There are a lot of women here in the Crescent City who need saving, but I'm not one of them. I appreciate what you were trying to do, but I can handle it." Because of her age, some of the other agents treated her as if she were a fragile female in need of saving. Lanier had to work twice as hard to prove she belonged with the FBI and that she was just as good as any of her male counterparts.

"I figured since I was there, I'd check out the area."

"Did you notice anything strange?" Lanier asked.

"No, nothing at all," he responded. "Things were pretty slow for about an hour after you arrived, then started to get busier toward midnight, but tapered off after that."

Lanier sat down in the empty chair facing him, then took a sip of her coffee. "Maybe I imagined it. Usually, my instincts are on point."

"Then trust your gut," he responded. "Let's assume you're right about this. Why do you think someone would be following you?"

"To scare me, I guess. Maybe to try to throw me off my game." Shrugging nonchalantly, Lanier picked up a yellow highlighter from the pencil cup on Daniel's desk. "Whoever it is doesn't know me, though. It'll take much more than that to frighten me."

"I'm sure I don't have to say this, but I'm gonna say it anyway. Be careful, Lanier."

"You too," she responded.

Lanier bit back a smile when his eyebrows rose a fraction. But Daniel could be in just as much danger. They all had to be careful because they had no idea who they were dealing with.

Humming softly, she strolled back to her office, pausing briefly to chat with a female officer. She could still feel Daniel's gaze on her. She couldn't explain it, but she kind of liked that he was watchful of her.

There was no harm in that. Daniel appeared to be a nice enough man with a pleasant personality. She could tell he genuinely cared about people. He greeted everyone, and it wasn't just his Southern charm—it was a facet of his personality.

Daniel possessed the qualities of a protector. He seemed always ready to lend a helping hand. His power was grounded in the desire to be his very best. She knew he had strong convictions and beliefs and would never compromise his ideals. She admired those qualities in Daniel. She respected him and felt drawn to him in a way she had never been drawn to any man.

From where he was seated, he had a clear view of Lanier in her temporary office. Daniel continued to quietly observe her while she worked. He admired her quiet confidence and fearless attitude. He found himself studying her profile. Everything about her intrigued him, even the air of mystery that seemed to surround her.

Sitting down at the desk that faced his partner's, Michael asked, "Do you think someone actually tailed Lanier the other night, or could it be her imagination?"

"I believe her," Daniel responded without so much as a second thought. He couldn't fully explain it, but he found Lanier to be credible in her observations.

Michael gave him a knowing look. "You followed her to the hotel last night, didn't you?"

Daniel tilted his head. "I wanted to make sure she was safe. She's a guest in our city."

"I'd say Agent Barrow looks pretty capable of handling herself."

"I know." He nodded. "But ambition can make a person careless. She's a high achiever. Lanier says this is all about justice for her, but I'm sure she also wants to make a name for herself by solving these cases. *I get it.* She's young, and this is about her future with the FBI."

"We have that in common, don't you think?" Michael suggested. "We want to be the detectives who solve this case. You know what it would mean for our careers."

"Actually, I just want to make sure my city is safe again," Daniel stated. "That's my only agenda."

"I know you don't care about recognition, but still… this could mean a promotion for you. You wanted to be captain."

Daniel cocked his head to one side. "That doesn't matter to me anymore, Michael. I just want to catch this evil murderer. He's a plague on this city." There was a time when he'd considered himself invincible, but almost dying changed him in many ways. That experience motivated Daniel to surrender his control and humble himself before the Lord. He believed this shift made him a much better person spiritually and professionally.

He caught sight of Lanier when she was in the evidence room. Daniel couldn't deny there was something special about her, but he chose instead to try to ignore whatever he was feeling.

Because it would not serve him well.

Chapter Six

By the time Friday rolled around, Lanier was more than ready for the weekend. Her fingers stung from the numerous paper cuts she'd acquired going through the boxes of old files.

"What plans do you have for this evening?" Daniel asked as they prepared to leave the station.

Lanier had a plan and hoped he'd join her. He'd mentioned earlier that he normally didn't work weekends unless he was on call, so she said, "I was thinking of canvassing some of the bars and clubs that each of the victims frequented. It's hard to know what to look for because they didn't go to the same ones. However, all the victims were patrons of Stephanie's Jazz Club."

"Do you want some company?" His eyes had a sheen of purpose in them.

"I have to say that you don't look like you're the clubbing type of guy," Lanier noted with amusement. "You might stick out like a sore thumb."

"I might, but when I'm conducting an investigation, I go wherever the trail leads me."

She smiled, grateful that she didn't have to check out

these places alone. "We have that in common. Why don't you meet me at Stephanie's Jazz Club around seven? We can start there. Oh, and don't drive the cop car," she teased. "You don't want to draw that kind of attention to yourself."

He grinned. "I'll see you then."

Lanier awarded him another smile. "Looking forward to it."

They walked out of the station together to their vehicles. She knew without glancing in his direction that Daniel waited in his car for her to leave. Lanier waved to him before driving away, and he waved back. Knowing he'd waited for her to pull out first sent a flutter through her. She drove out of the parking lot and merged into the flow of traffic.

Lanier had never felt anything close to this, nor had she ever expected to feel such fondness for him. She'd always been able to stifle her feelings in the past. She pushed the troubling thought to the back of her mind for now. She had work to do.

Later, in her suite, Lanier tried on several different outfits. She chose a silver sequined dress that looked nice on her but successfully hid the pistol strapped to her thigh. Her clutch purse wasn't large enough to conceal a weapon. Her long dark hair hung in loose curls instead of the tight bun she wore during the workday.

Lanier was on alert as she navigated to her vehicle.

Her cell phone rang just as soon as she was inside the car.

It was her best friend. "Celine…hey girl…"

"I hope you're finding some time to enjoy the fabulous city of New Orleans."

Lanier grinned. "I told you I'm just here to work. This investigation is keeping me quite busy."

"I going to be there in a couple of weeks for a conference, but I'll be free on Sunday. Please tell me you'll take some time off to just hang out. I seriously need some female bonding time."

"I'm in the middle of a high-profile case, but I'll do what I can to make sure we get together," she promised. "Even if it's just for a meal."

"I'll get back to you when I make my plane reservations."

Lanier was excited over the idea of Celine coming to town. "I'm about to go out in a few, but I'll call you tomorrow. We can go over all the details then."

"I'm glad to hear you're going out. Is it a date?" Celine asked.

"No, it's work," Lanier replied. "I have to go, but we'll talk later."

She was running a few minutes behind because of Celine's call but wasn't worried. The hotel wasn't that far from the club.

Lanier broke into a tiny smile when she glimpsed Daniel sitting at the bar. She sauntered toward him, knowing she'd caught the eye of most of the men in the club. It was intentional on her part. She was trying to catch a killer.

"Anyone sitting here?" she asked Daniel, speaking loudly to be heard over the music.

"No, the chair is yours," he responded.

To an outsider, Lanier and Daniel looked like two people just meeting. They didn't want anyone to get the idea that they were together. It was meant to look as if they'd just met.

He bought her a soda, and she pretended to flirt with him, although it wasn't hard to do. Daniel's appeal was devastating.

She leaned toward him and whispered, "I haven't noticed anything out of the ordinary here so far, but I want to stay for a few minutes more."

"Same here," he whispered back.

Daniel's cologne assaulted her senses. He was so very handsome, and Lanier reacted strongly to him, although she tried to fight against it. She couldn't allow whatever she was feeling to get out of control. To do so would potentially open Lanier to losing her heart to a man she could never have a future with.

When Lanier had first walked into the club, it took a minute for Daniel to remember to breathe and find his voice. Lanier was stunning. He was sure every man in the room thought so.

Just as they were about to leave, a man approached her, saying, "Hey beautiful… I saw you walk in, and I just knew you were the lady for me."

She awarded him a polite smile. "Thank you for the compliment, but I'm not interested."

"How do you know? You haven't even gotten to know me yet."

Daniel itched to intervene but held his peace. Lanier would signal if she needed his assistance.

She looked straight at the guy. "I'm sure there are several women here tonight who'd love to talk to you— I'm just not one of them. You're standing here wasting time with me while that woman over there, the one in red, has been watching you this whole time."

He followed her gaze, then looked back at Lanier. "Enjoy your evening."

Daniel liked that Lanier was direct without being rude.

He signaled the bartender. "Put her drink on my tab, then bring me the check, please."

She pointed to his glass. "What are you drinking?"

"Pepsi. I don't drink alcohol."

"Neither do I," she responded.

They finished their drinks. Lanier was the first to get up and walk out, the heels of her shoes clapping to the beat of the music playing in the background.

After he paid the bill, Daniel joined her outside.

"All the victims came here, but there wasn't anything remarkable about it. I noticed there was a lot of steady traffic. I initially thought it would be more off the beaten path. Carolyn left here and went to another club, right?"

Daniel nodded. "She and her friends went to this hole-in-the-wall blues joint on Bayou Road."

"I'll meet you there," Lanier said, unlocking her car door.

He followed her in his truck.

"The person we're looking for most likely knows who we are," Daniel said when they arrived at the second club. "We can assume he knows our every move—which is how he's able to stay a step ahead of us. Canvassing these clubs may only deter him from attacking another woman, or it might cause him to escalate things."

"Until now, he's never felt threatened," Lanier stated. "Maybe seeing us will force him to make a move."

"I hope you're right," Daniel said.

"He's been in control," she stated. "But we're changing the narrative."

* * *

At the next club, the music was loud and thumping throughout the building. Daniel could almost see the walls move, but it was a trick of the eye due to the strobe lights. He and Lanier navigated slowly, wading through the sea of men and women, and making a beeline for an empty booth, which would provide a perfect view of every area of the club.

"This is definitely a different type of crowd," Lanier said when they sat down. This group was younger and more carefree, whereas the people at Stephanie's were more sophisticated. It seemed more suited to couples.

Daniel's gaze traveled the room. The music seemed to be a drug, taking people higher and higher. The entire atmosphere buzzed with energy.

"Dance with me," Lanier said, shocking him.

"I grew up with a preacher for a dad, and he didn't allow us to listen to secular music or dance."

Her eyebrows rose in surprise. "So you've never danced? Not even in your room alone?"

"I don't dance. Not sure I even have rhythm." Daniel glanced at the dance floor and the sea of people already on it. "Besides, there's no room."

"C'mon…" She took his hand, leading him to the dance floor. "Just sway from side to side. I want to get next to that guy out there in the black shirt and pants. I've been watching him for a few minutes, and he fits the profile."

Lanier moved in her dress, the sequins catching the strobe light spinning above, projecting every shade of the rainbow against the walls.

"There are cameras everywhere. It's too risky," Daniel stated after a while. "But our perp seems to like a challenge."

"I don't know. He may be more of a lurker in the shadows," Lanier responded. "A spectator. Let's check out one more place, and then we can call it a night," she suggested. "I want to go to the bar where Gayle Giraud worked. She was attacked leaving the bar and the only one killed in an outside location. The unsub acted impulsively and without a plan." She wanted to see the place where her mother once worked.

"What are you hoping to find there?" Daniel asked.

"I don't know…maybe a connection between the cold cases and the new string of victims. It's worth a look."

He gave a slight shrug. "Let's go."

Peppers was a small place tucked away in a remote area in Algiers.

"I'm definitely overdressed for this place," she said with a chuckle when they arrived. There wasn't much to it. Some of the paint was peeling off the walls. Overall, it had a seedy look.

Lanier couldn't imagine her mother working in a place like this. Maybe it hadn't looked so rundown twenty years ago.

"I don't think we'll be here too long," Daniel responded. "You go in first. I'll wait for about five minutes before I come inside."

Lanier got out of her car and strolled inside.

When Daniel entered, he found her sitting at a table near the heavily tinted storefront window.

He walked over and asked if he could join her.

Lanier nodded. "Sure."

When he sat down, she said, "I can't believe the bar is still open after all this time."

Daniel glanced around. "Yeah…this place has been around for a long time."

Lanier captured the faces of everyone there, imprinting them in her memory. Thankfully, the place could hold less than a hundred people, and there were only a few patrons still there at this late hour. The bartender had announced the last call just as they were entering.

Daniel eyed Lanier. She sat up straight, then said, "I feel like someone is watching us."

She waited a heartbeat before casually glancing around.

There was one man looking in her direction, but when their eyes met, he quickly turned away. There wasn't anything remarkable about him.

A server approached them.

"We're getting ready to leave," Daniel told her.

"Actually, I have a question," Lanier interjected. "When you leave here, does anyone walk you to your car as a safety measure?"

"My brother picks me up," the young woman responded. "He comes here every night I work. He's sitting over there at the end of the bar. He makes sure all the girls get to their cars safely."

"The reason I asked is because I noticed there weren't any cameras outside."

"Yeah, we keep asking the owner to put some out there, but he don't listen to us. A girl was attacked years ago but 'cause nothing bad has happened since then, I guess he ain't worried about it."

"Stay safe," Lanier told her.

They got up and left the bar.

"What do you know about this place?" she asked.

"It's a family-owned business. Been around for almost thirty years."

Swallowing her annoyance, she uttered, "I'm really amazed that after Gayle was kidnapped outside this bar—you'd think they would've installed security cameras around the building. At least to offer some protection for their employees." Lanier was disgusted.

Daniel nodded in agreement.

"I'm going to head to the hotel," Lanier said. "I can barely keep my eyes open, and some of this music is giving me a headache."

He chuckled. "Can't hang, huh?"

"Not tonight I can't." She unlocked her car door. "Thanks for being here."

"I couldn't let you go alone," he responded.

Lanier headed to the hotel. She stared through the windshield, her arm muscles tense as she gripped the wheel in frustration. Nothing had come out of canvassing the bars. *I did enjoy Daniel's company*, she decided. *So it wasn't a complete waste of time.*

When she was less than five minutes away from the hotel, Lanier pressed the accelerator and swerved around a slow-moving car.

Bright lights coming from her left caught her attention. An SUV had run the red light and was barreling toward her. Lanier gripped the steering wheel and tried not to panic.

The vehicle that hit her came out of nowhere. She didn't even have time to tap the gas pedal before she heard metal crunching.

Instinctively, Lanier put her foot on the brake.

The seat belt prevented her body from plunging forward through the windshield.

Shattered glass scattered across her field of vision as

the intensity of the airbag deploying smacked her in the face and knocked the wind out of her lungs.

Lanier valiantly fought against the darkness that threatened to surround her but quickly lost the battle.

Daniel felt a tightening in his stomach as the shrill sirens of an ambulance rushed past him in the opposite direction. He couldn't explain it, but he had a feeling Lanier was in trouble. It was a quick and disturbing thought.

He maneuvered around the cars in front of him, then found an opening to turn around.

Daniel rushed after the ambulance. As he got closer to the scene of the accident, a sense of dread flowed through him when he caught sight of the rental car Lanier had been driving at an odd angle in the middle of the street with the front end and driver's side door mangled.

He glanced around for the car that had collided into hers, but it wasn't there—only a couple of vehicles parked on the side of the road whose drivers may have witnessed the accident. Chunks of twisted metal and glass were strewn all over the ground.

A hit-and-run.

The muscles in his neck tensed up and his stomach clenched tightly as he parked his car and got out.

Daniel walked briskly over to one of the police officers and showed his badge. "I know the victim. She's FBI Special Agent Barrow."

The officer allowed him to approach the car, open the door and begin his assessment.

Lanier's eyes were closed, and blood was dripping from a laceration on her forehead. The airbag had deployed, leaving visible bruising to her face. A wave of apprehension swept through him seeing her unconscious, bruised and bleeding like this.

"Lanier…" he called her name gently, then stepped aside so the paramedics could work on her.

He knew instinctively that this was no simple hit-and-run. Someone had deliberately crashed into Lanier's car.

She was being targeted and would have to be extremely cautious until they found the killer.

Chapter Seven

Lanier woke up to the sound of a monitor beeping steadily and voices coming from the hallway. Every now and then a code was announced over the intercom, or an alarm went off whenever a medicine or saline bag needed attention. When she opened her eyes, her vision was a bit fuzzy. She blinked a few times to clear it up.

Pain exploded out of nowhere. Her face and chest felt as if they were on fire. Lanier moaned in agony. Her body stiffened and tensed up, fighting against the discomfort.

"You're awake."

She turned her head in the direction the voice had come from.

Daniel stood near the door, his expression one of concern.

She groggily accessed her surroundings. "I'm in a hospital?"

He nodded, then walked into the room and stood at the foot of the bed. "You were in a car accident."

Lanier took a deep breath and tried to focus her thoughts.

The memory of what happened invaded the forefront of her mind. "I remember…someone crashed into me," she stated.

"I don't suppose you remember anything about the car."

She shook her head, then winced, lightly touching the bandage on her forehead. "It happened so fast. The only thing I know is that it was some type of SUV. The windows were tinted… That's all I remember."

Lanier tried to sit up, but the burning pain overtook her. She wasn't going to let it stop her, though. "I have to get out of here."

She tried once more to sit up and get out of the hospital bed, but Daniel stopped her. "The doctor wants to keep you overnight." His tone was firm and exacting.

Her vision gradually cleared, and Lanier was able to meet his gaze. Annoyed, she responded, "I'm a little banged up, but I'm fine, Daniel. We have work to do. I can't lay around in this bed while we have a killer on the streets."

When she attempted to sit up a third time, her head throbbed with pain. A soft moan escaped her lips.

The pillow was much too soft, and her head and body ached with every movement.

"Just lie there, Lanier. You need to rest."

"Daniel, what I *need* is to get out there and look for whoever hit me. I want to go back to collect evidence. That driver wanted me dead or seriously hurt."

"Michael's already on it," he assured her. "He's looking into it."

Lanier turned her head away from Daniel, squeezing her eyes shut to block out the pain.

"You're hurting."

"My head and my ribs."

A nurse entered the room. "How're you feeling?"

"I have a headache...more like a migraine," Lanier responded. "And pain in my chest. I assume it's from the airbag." Her whole body was sore, but she didn't complain. She didn't want to show any vulnerability in front of Daniel. These types of incidents came with her job, and she could handle it.

Nodding, the nurse said, "I'll get you something for the pain. You'll probably be sore for a few days."

She left and returned with a small cup of pills and poured Lanier some water.

Lanier hated the chalky taste but could endure it if it would ease her pain.

"You get some rest," Daniel said. "I'll be outside."

"If you plan on keeping watch outside my door, you might as well stay in here with me," Lanier stated.

Daniel's gaze locked into hers. "You don't have to worry."

"You misunderstood. I'm not worried about being attacked here in the hospital. I'm getting out of here in the morning. *I'll need a ride.*"

He chuckled. "Sure. I'll give you that ride."

"If the accident was intentional, then we can assume that I've definitely gotten the unsub's attention."

"If that's true...it could've cost you your life, Lanier. Michael suggested we give you protection. He offered to stay here, but I told him I'd stay. He's got the kids, you know..."

"Of course. He should be home with them," Lanier agreed. "I'm probably safer in this hospital room than anywhere else."

"I knew you'd say that." Daniel rubbed his hand on the back of his neck.

"I have you and Michael watching my back. I couldn't be any safer."

Lanier was grateful he was there with her. That he'd thought to come check up on her confirmed what she already knew about him. Daniel Jordan was compassionate, and she liked this about him.

Daniel sat down on the convertible sofa in Lanier's hospital room. She fell asleep shortly after the nurse gave her the pain medication.

He tossed his jacket onto the other chair in the room but couldn't sit still. Things could've gone bad tonight. Lanier Barrow could've died. He felt the familiar stirrings of rage. He settled against the cushion of the sofa and closed his eyes, forcing his body to relax. His hands were clenched into fists.

Daniel unclenched them and sent up a silent prayer of thanks. He was grateful that God had spared her life.

There were still some things gnawing at him. Was this just an accident? If not, how did the perp know how to get to Lanier so easily? Was he somehow tracking her? He sent a text to Michael.

Daniel: Hey, have techs check for some type of tracking device on the rental.

Michael: Okay. How is Lanier?

Daniel: Bruised and in some pain. Thanks.

Daniel didn't believe in coincidences. First, someone watching her at the hotel and now a hit and run… he preferred to err on the side of caution. They couldn't afford to underestimate the person they were looking for—this perp was well trained and able to fade easily into the night. Who could it be? Someone clearly didn't want Lanier investigating any further than she already had. But why target her and not him and Michael, too?

He didn't like this helpless feeling. Daniel was more determined than ever to find the murderer and put this investigation behind him. "I'm going to find you," he whispered.

Daniel drifted off to sleep.

He woke up five hours later to find Lanier walking out of the bathroom. She'd showered and was dressed in a pair of leggings and a sweatshirt.

"Good morning," she greeted him.

"What are you doing?"

"I'm getting ready to leave. As soon as the doctor comes, I'm getting out of here."

Daniel gestured to her outfit. "Where'd you get that?"

"I always keep a spare outfit in my tote. Thanks for taking it out of the car for me. I almost took it to my suite, but I decided to just leave it in the car. Good thing I did."

Daniel wasn't surprised that Lanier seemed to be prepared for the unexpected. She was always thinking ahead, and he appreciated this quality in her. It was something they had in common. He kept an extra set of shirts and slacks in his vehicle as well.

When the doctor arrived, Daniel stepped outside of the room to give Lanier some privacy.

He didn't return until she was alone.

"I'm free," she said with a tentative smile.

"I'm taking you straight to the hotel," Daniel stated. "I don't expect to see you at the station at all this week."

"I'm in no mood to argue with you right now."

The nurse arrived with a wheelchair.

"I don't need that," Lanier uttered. "I can walk to the car."

Daniel gave the woman a sympathetic smile. "I'll pull my car around to the exit doors. See you downstairs."

"That man…" Lanier huffed.

"Cares a great deal about you," he overheard the nurse respond as she assisted Lanier into the chair and wheeled her downstairs, where he would be waiting.

He took the elevator down to the first floor, then strode briskly through the exit doors and toward the parking lot.

After he pulled his car up, Daniel got out of the vehicle, walked around to open the passenger door for her, then helped her onto the seat.

A few minutes later, Daniel pulled into a parking spot at the hotel and helped her upstairs to her suite. Lanier looked a bit unsteady on her feet and probably couldn't wait to reach the bedroom. He assisted her into bed, then said, "I'll pick up your prescription and something for you to eat."

"Thank you," she murmured. "Take my key with you. I think I'm going to try and get some real sleep. The nurses kept waking me up all through the night."

"Get some rest."

Daniel walked quietly out of the room and made his way to the door. He made sure to put out the Do Not Disturb hanger on the knob.

He wasn't gone long, and Lanier was still sleeping when he returned. He placed the bottle of pills on the nightstand and the food in the mini-fridge, then left. He planned to call her later in the day to see how she was faring and if she needed anything.

If the killer was going to target Lanier, it wasn't going to be while Daniel was around.

Lanier was seated at her desk when Daniel arrived to work on Wednesday. He eyed the Band-Aid covering the stitches on her forehead, and the fading bruises on her face. "What are you doing here?"

"Good morning to you, too," she responded as casually as she could manage.

"I thought you were taking a few days off."

"I stayed home Monday and Tuesday," Lanier said. "We have a lot of work to do, so I don't have the luxury of lying around and doing nothing." Daniel was under just as much pressure to find the killer, so he should understand her need to get back to the investigation.

Michael arrived minutes after. He paused in his tracks when he saw Lanier. "Shouldn't you be in bed resting?"

She released a frustrated sigh. "You two are worse than one helicopter mom. *I'm fine.*"

Michael glanced at Daniel before heading to the break room to grab a cup of coffee.

She winced and tenderly touched her forehead.

"Are you sure you're up to this?"

"Stop with all this fuss over a few cuts and bruises. I'm a little sore, but I'm good for the most part." Softening her tone, Lanier added, "I do appreciate your concern, though."

Michael stuck his head inside. "C'mon, Daniel... Lanier's got this."

He nodded and left her office, but then returned with the first aid kit. Daniel handed her a packet containing Tylenol. "These should help with the pain."

"Thanks, Dad..." Lanier swallowed the two pills,

followed by half a bottle of water. *"Can we get to work now?"* She was touched by the gesture but cautioned herself not to read too much into it.

"Sure." Daniel walked to the door and gestured for Michael to join them.

Bracing herself against the discomfort, Lanier pointed to a notebook filled with notes. "Before we get to the murder investigations—Michael, did you find anything at the site of the accident?"

He nodded. "I sent fragments from the windshield, headlights and metal of the car that hit you to our labs."

"Thanks." Lanier smiled and took a sip of water from a plastic bottle. "I've reviewed most of the cold case files and what we know of the recent murders," she said. "The unsub is working to make it *look* like the women are randomly selected, but he's trying to achieve a certain result when he kills."

"I still think we have a copycat killer on our hands," Michael stated. "It's not the Crescent City Strangler."

"I've kept an open mind since you arrived, Lanier, but I just don't see a connection to the cold cases," Daniel said. "Because there isn't one. I have to agree with Michael. This isn't the Crescent City Strangler."

"Oh, there is a connection," she countered. "Earlier today, I spoke with a friend in the FBI forensics lab. I had CSI send him some of the rope samples that were found on your first body. That sample is an *exact* match to the sample that was used to kill Anna Jacobs and Gayle Giraud. I believe the fiber found on this last victim will also be a match."

Both Daniel and Michael looked surprised.

"That rope would have to be at least twenty years old. It only has a life span of ten at most," Daniel responded.

"If someone plans on going rock climbing with it, you're right. However, when it comes to strangling someone with a garrote…it's a different thing altogether." Lanier paused a moment, then asked, "Do you still believe there are two different unsubs?"

Daniel and Michael exchanged looks but didn't respond.

She assumed from their lack of response that they were still digesting the news that they were looking for the Crescent City Strangler.

After they left her office, Lanier performed a search to get a list of SUVs currently being serviced in repair shops in New Orleans and surrounding cities.

She wasn't entirely convinced that she'd been hit by some random driver. If she was right, then this meant that the killer was getting desperate.

And desperate people often make mistakes.

Lanier had discovered a link between the cold case and recent murders.

Rope.

Daniel's worst fears were now confirmed. The Crescent City Strangler had come out of retirement. He raised his eyes heavenward and whispered a silent prayer, asking for help in solving this case.

"What are you thinking about?" Michael asked.

"I don't know. I never really considered the possibility that Lanier's theory had merit." Daniel eyed his partner. "My gut kept telling me that we were looking for someone new, but that rope being a match… I hadn't thought to have the fibers tested against the evidence in the cold cases. Mainly because the rope used twenty years ago just seemed too far-fetched."

Accepting a folder from an officer passing by, Michael uttered, "I never saw that coming either, but in our defense, we hadn't really looked into the cold cases. We were sure that we had another killer." He walked back toward his office.

Daniel stole a peek at Lanier once they were alone. Her shoulders had relaxed, he saw, and she'd lost some of the pain lines around her mouth.

Good. The Tylenol seems to have helped.

Daniel decided he needed to get some air. He pulled out a pair of walking shoes from a box under his desk.

"Are you about to go on one of your walks?" Lanier asked as she approached his desk.

"Actually, I am. It's a stress reliever for me."

She smiled. "Exercise relieves my stress as well, only I enjoy doing it in an air-conditioned gym."

Daniel chuckled. "I take it you're not an outdoors type of girl."

"I enjoy a bike ride every now and then, but when it comes to exercise—I prefer the indoors."

"I love being outside," he said. "Nothing like fresh air."

"That's true," she responded. "This is the perfect weather for it, too."

"I'll be gone for about twenty minutes."

"Daniel…"

He paused in his tracks. "Yes…"

"I can tell I blindsided you and Michael earlier."

"That you did. Twenty-year-old rope…" Daniel shook his head. *"He's really back."* The idea sent a wave of dread flowing through him. He hoped to keep the news under wraps for a little while longer.

"I'm afraid so," Lanier responded. "But we're going to find the unsub this time."

"I don't want this getting out to the news outlets just yet."

"Glad to hear that," she murmured. "We still need to dig deeper to find out why he chose these four women other than the fact that they were married and enjoyed going out on the weekends."

"The question comes back to, 'Why them?'" Daniel said.

"We're going to find the answer. We won't stop until we do," Lanier assured him.

Daniel didn't know why, but he believed her.

Chapter Eight

At the end of the workday, Lanier couldn't wait to slip into the sudsy bathwater. She hoped the hot temperature would melt away the aches and pains infiltrating her body. She laid her head back, eyes closed, soaking away the drudgeries of the day.

Daniel said she'd come back to work too soon. He was probably right, but Lanier would never admit this to him. Her pride forced her to suffer through the day in silence, but now she released the groans aloud in the privacy of her suite.

Lanier got up, stepped out of the tub, and dried off with a thick, fluffy towel. She slipped on a pair of gray sweats and a blue T-shirt emblazoned with the letters FBI.

She ordered room service, then gingerly settled down on the sofa to review more of the files and evidence collected from the cold cases as she waited for her dinner to arrive. Lanier struggled to find a position in which she didn't feel pain. It wasn't as bad as it had been, but the throbbing was still a constant reminder of the accident.

The knock on her door took Lanier's attention from her reading.

She stood up and walked briskly to the door, then held it open so the server could bring in her meal on a cart.

"Thank you," she murmured as she signed the check.

Lanier sat at the dining table to enjoy her food and turned on the television to watch the news as she ate.

When she finished, Lanier returned to the sofa and back to the file she'd been reading. She hoped reviewing the notes of the Crescent City Strangler's first victim would give her some insight into the unsub. Lanier wanted more than anything to find the killer. Only then would she be able to finally continue the path she was meant to walk. Her desire was to go back to school, obtain a law degree and become a district attorney. She possessed no lack of faith in closing this case; however, there were moments when doubt tried to creep in.

Lanier took a couple of pills to help with the pain, then lay back, waiting for them to work their magic.

Her phone vibrated.

It was a text message.

Daniel: Hey. Just wanted to check on you. If you're not feeling up to it tomorrow, please stay home. I'll update you if anything comes up.

Lanier: Thank you for your concern. Good night, Dad :)

Daniel: LOL

Smiling, Lanier closed her eyes once more as sleep sought to claim her. He was sweet to be so concerned about her. If this was a different life, maybe she and Daniel…

She didn't finish the thought before falling asleep.

Daniel was the first to arrive at the station early Monday morning. His alarm pulled him from what little sleep he could get. He was the detective on call all weekend and thankfully, it wasn't a busy one. He handed off most of his cases to other detectives in the office because the Crescent City Strangler murders demanded his full attention. He wasn't going to get much rest until the killer was apprehended.

Thanksgiving was Thursday, and Daniel had been looking forward to spending the holiday with his mother and other family members. This year the dinner would be hosted by his aunt, who lived in Houston. He and his mother had originally planned to leave on Wednesday evening after his shift ended, but now, deep in the investigation, Daniel decided it was best that he stay in town.

He picked up the phone and dialed his mother's number.

"Hey son…"

"Mom, you're gonna have to go to Houston alone. I need to stay here."

"I had a feeling this would happen."

"I'm sorry."

"It's not your fault, Daniel. I know you have a job to do."

"I'll take you to the airport."

"I can get my neighbor to take me, son."

"No, I want to see you off," he insisted. "I'll be there a couple of hours before the flight. I appreciate you being so understanding, Mom."

Just as he hung up, a couple of patrol officers arrived to start the workday. Daniel decided he did not miss wearing a uniform when the weather was eighty degrees or more, but this fall weather was perfect: not too hot or too cold. The one thing Daniel was sure about was that he loved his job—most of the time.

His partner entered through the doors of the homicide division. "How was it over the weekend?" Michael inquired.

Daniel picked up a pen and opened a file. "Not one call, for which I'm grateful."

Michael stifled a yawn. "Sorry. I was up late working on my son's science project last night. Of course, he waited until the last minute to tell me it was due today."

Daniel laughed in commiseration as they navigated to the break room for coffee.

When Daniel returned to his desk, Lanier had arrived. Her bruises were fading nicely from the hit-and-run. They greeted one another, and inside her office, Lanier removed her coat and took a seat at her desk.

Daniel forced himself to look away, gather himself and focus on his work.

"Are you developing feelings for Lanier?" Michael asked from the doorway of the break room.

"Why would you ask me that?" Daniel responded. He was glad he was the only one in there now.

Michael gave him a pointed look. Then his gaze traveled to Lanier's office. "I know you, remember."

His partner must've caught him watching her. "I'm not that person anymore," Daniel stated. "After LaVerne, my feelings on dating coworkers changed. That includes Lanier. She is FBI, but still off-limits. Let's just focus on our job right now." He made a vow that he'd never let his personal relationships affect his professional life again.

An hour later, Daniel sat alone in a conference room, reviewing the autopsy results of each of the four women. He wanted to be free from any distractions such as phone calls, conversations and people in general. Lanier was in her office doing the same. They'd decided to read them separately, then discuss their notes and findings later.

Two hours had passed when he finally emerged from the room. Daniel stopped by Lanier's office and said, "I'm about to grab some lunch. Would you like to join me?"

She didn't hesitate in her response. "Sure."

"I thought we'd eat out."

Lanier seemed surprised. "You didn't bring your lunch today?"

"I didn't." Daniel smiled. "I do eat out occasionally. Everyone thinks I'm frugal, but the truth is that I much prefer home-cooked meals."

They decided to eat at a little restaurant called the Velvet Cactus on Argonne Boulevard.

"This is another of my favorite places to eat," Daniel said.

"I love Mexican food, so this is right up my alley." Lanier glanced around the dining area, then said, "I noticed that the overall conditions of the bodies of the four women were considered unremarkable outside of a crushed larynx. No illegal drugs, alcohol content at a legal level. Four very healthy women murdered by a ruthless killer."

He nodded in agreement. "I noticed the same. According to the toxicology results, only one of the women took prescription medicine."

"They weren't women who abused drugs or even smoked cigarettes," Lanier said. "They seemed to take care of themselves when it came to their health. This tells me that the unsub is very intentional in his selection of victims."

"He must get to know them on some level," Daniel responded.

She agreed. "Which means he's not just grabbing random women off the streets. The unsub has had some interaction with them."

When their food arrived, Lanier stated, "You seem to enjoy your job, Daniel." She nibbled on chicken nachos, while he'd chosen the chicken flautas. "I've never seen you come to work with a look of dread that some people have when they hate their jobs."

"I love my work," Daniel responded. "My only real disappointment was when I wasn't assigned the brand-new Charger. Instead, they gave me this six-year-old Impala to drive."

Lanier gave a tiny smile. "I'd want the Dodge Charger, too. In fact, that's what I bought."

He leaned back in his chair. "I'm not really surprised to hear this. I bet it's black on black."

Grinning, she responded, "You'd be correct."

"I've been thinking of getting one myself."

Lanier studied him. "I see you with maybe black on black or black with a gray interior."

Daniel gave her a handsome smile. "Yep...that sounds like me."

He helped her finish her nachos.

"When we leave here, I'll drop you back off at the station. Michael and I have to meet with a couple of witnesses for an unrelated case," Daniel announced. "We're so close to closing this one—I didn't want to hand it off."

"Recorded interviews?" Lanier inquired.

He nodded. "Hopefully we'll get information that confirms what we already know from the evidence to finally put all the pieces of the puzzle together."

"I don't know about you, but I find it frustrating when the witnesses attempt to make sense of what they saw after the fact. The challenge is that we have to separate the facts from speculation."

Daniel gave a slight nod in agreement.

"Are there any parts of your job that you dislike?" Daniel asked her.

Lanier nodded. "I have moments when I believe that the justice system is broken—that innocent people aren't protected. It seems like evil wins most of the time. That's one of the reasons I became an FBI agent. I wanted to help balance the scales."

He could understand her being disillusioned at times, but Daniel hoped she wouldn't continue to feel this way. He wiped his mouth on his napkin. "I believe that justice *will* prevail, and that the world is filled with good people, despite all the terrible things that happen."

"Is this why you became a police officer?" Lanier asked.

"My reason isn't so different from yours," he responded. "I want to ensure that the people responsible for committing crimes are caught and prosecuted to the full extent of the law."

Daniel checked his watch. "We'd better get going."

He dropped Lanier back at the station before he and Michael left again.

"I'm not blind," Michael said when they exited the parking lot. "You're attracted to Lanier."

Daniel gave a short chuckle. "What are you talking about?"

"It's me... Michael..."

"It doesn't mean anything," Daniel said. "We work together."

"And?"

"That's all that can come of it." His partner was right. He felt the nauseating sinking of despair and disappointment.

"The heart wants what the heart wants, Daniel," Michael stated. "That's all I'll say on the matter."

He felt an acute sense of loss. "You've said more than enough."

Daniel parked the vehicle and got out. "Let's hope this doesn't turn out to be a waste of our time."

A couple of women had come forward as witnesses to a shooting that had taken place a few weeks ago. He and Michael were there to find out what they saw and whether the information would prove to be reliable.

They made it back to the station just as Lanier was leaving for the day.

"I'll see y'all tomorrow," she said. "It's been a long day."

Daniel was already missing that beautiful smile of hers. He wasn't looking forward to the day when this case was closed, and she had to return to Virginia.

June Barrow called to wish her niece a happy Thanksgiving. "I really wish you could've come home."

"I do, too, but this investigation needs my full attention."

"How are you doing with the investigation?" June inquired. "Any news on my sister's death?"

"Nothing new, Auntie. But don't worry…it's going well. We're going to find the Crescent City Strangler. And when we do, we'll get justice for my mother and the other women." Lanier thought it best to not mention the hit-and-run accident to her aunt and uncle. She didn't want them to worry about her. "What are you planning to cook?"

"Cajun turkey with oyster dressing, string beans, candied yams, macaroni and cheese."

"Sounds great. Where's Uncle?"

"He should be home shortly," June responded. "I asked him to stop at the grocery store to pick up some items I forgot. How does it feel being back in New Orleans?"

"Different," Lanier responded. "I went by Nana's house. I wasn't sure what to expect, but it's still standing. What's left of it, anyway."

"Are you sure nobody knows who you are?"

"My secret is safe, Auntie," she assured June. "The detectives I'm working with have no idea that Gayle Giraud is my mother. I'll only tell them when it's absolutely necessary."

"I just heard the garage door. Your uncle's home," June said. "I better help him with the shopping bags. You know he bought more than I asked for—he can never keep to the list."

Lanier chuckled. "You're right about that. Call me back once you two get settled."

"Give me about fifteen minutes."

While she waited for her aunt to call, she got dressed. Lanier was going to spend the rest of the holiday working.

It was almost noon when she walked into the police station. Daniel was already there and working in a conference room.

"Great way to spend Thanksgiving," he said when she approached him.

"Especially when there's a killer on the loose," Lanier responded as she took a seat across from him. "Did you have a chance to review the file on Gayle Giraud?"

"I did."

"Do you still think she was a stripper?"

"According to witness statements, she was a student and worked as a bartender—just as you said. I don't understand why he chose her..." Daniel stared off into space while twirling the pen in his hand. "She was assaulted outdoors...everything about this case is different from the other victims back then."

"Maybe it was a case of mistaken identity," Lanier suggested. "He killed the wrong girl, and that's what stopped him."

"So why did he start up again? What could've triggered him?" Daniel asked.

"That's what we have to find out."

Sighing, Daniel said, "It angers me that all these women were murdered by someone acting as judge and jury."

"I feel the same way," she responded. "It makes me that much more determined to find the unsub. He needs to be put away once and for all. Gayle Giraud and the rest of the victims deserve justice."

He nodded in agreement. "We're going to do everything possible to make that happen."

Lanier picked up a thick notebook. "Did you get a chance to look at this one? It's Anna Jacobs's murder book."

It was back to work as normal on Friday morning.

Daniel trudged in, wishing he'd been able to take a couple days off, although criminals never seemed to take a break.

His mood shifted to buoyant when Lanier arrived. She strolled in wearing a red turtleneck and charcoal-gray pants beneath a black leather jacket. Her hair was in a ponytail.

Lanier greeted him with a smile. "Good morning, Daniel."

"Did you find any good Black Friday deals?" he asked. "I figured you'd spent your morning shopping."

"I found a couple online. I'm not really a mall person." Lanier removed her coat. "I'm going to make some coffee. You want a cup?"

"I thought you normally had tea in the mornings?"

"I switch it up sometimes," she said. "Depends on how well I slept the night before. It took me a while to fall asleep after I got home last night, so I need coffee."

"Everything okay?"

Lanier nodded. "Yeah. I'm fine. Just kept thinking about the Thanksgiving meal last year. The turkey sandwich I ordered last night just didn't cut it for me."

"You miss your family."

She looked him straight in the face. "I didn't realize just how much."

They chatted for a few more minutes before Lanier settled in her office.

When Michael arrived, he and Daniel went to join the other detectives in a short meeting.

The precinct was quiet for the most part. A few calls came in, but nothing for the homicide division, allowing Daniel to get caught up on paperwork and follow up on his open cases.

Every now and then he would glance up to see what Lanier was doing. She appeared deep in thought as she audited several of the cold case files. The more time they spent together, the more Daniel felt a tangible bond forming between them—and he was powerless to resist it.

His phone rang. After he talked to the caller, Daniel joined Lanier in her office.

She glanced up at him and asked, "Are you okay? Did something happen?"

Daniel felt a flick of emotion cross his face. "I just got a call from the mother of one of the victims. It's always hard when family members call you, desperate for answers. Sometimes they call or come to the station with what they believe are leads and evidence when it turns out to be nothing..." Daniel gave a shake of his head. "I feel like I'm failing them despite doing everything I can to get them answers."

"I understand completely," she said. "It's hard when you can't offer the family anything promising. I do everything I can to let them know that I really do care about the victim and finding the person responsible." Lanier settled back in her chair. "I'm sure they know you're doing your best."

Daniel sat down in the chair facing her. "Some days

it's hard to do this job. Like right now, with women going missing and ending up murdered. I keep praying for some type of breakthrough to help us find this killer. I want to be the one who prevents it from happening again."

When Lanier saw the look in his eyes, her feelings shifted. She was drawn to him, despite the fears that never went away. The intense pain over losing her mother and grandmother served as a barricade around her heart. Lanier didn't want to love so hard because she couldn't handle losing someone else, but somehow Daniel managed to break through.

"You're a very interesting man, Daniel Jordan," Lanier said after a moment. "I like working with you."

"I can say the same," he responded with a smile.

Lanier forced her attention away from his perfectly shaped lips. She didn't want to go down that road. Because when the investigation was over, Lanier would return to Virginia and the bureau. Their paths might not ever cross again.

The thought made her sad.

Daniel sensed something was bothering Lanier a few days later, but he couldn't figure out what it could be. He hadn't experienced such a strong connection to a woman in a very long time.

As the day wore on, Lanier seemed more relaxed. There was a glow in her eyes that hadn't been there before. This case had consumed both of their lives, but Daniel hoped it would be over soon. He didn't want to pry, but felt compelled to ask, "Are you okay?"

"Today is my mother's birthday. She's been gone a long time, but I'm really missing her."

He wanted to embrace Lanier, to offer some comfort, but he didn't want her or any of his coworkers to mis-read the gesture. "I'm sorry."

She gave him a brief smile. "Thank you. I'm fine. I just need to stay busy."

He glanced down at the stack of files on her desk. "As long as the Crescent City Strangler is out there—we have a lot to do."

"You're right about that," Lanier responded. "I'm compiling a list of family members to interview."

"The ones from the cold cases?"

She nodded. "I'm hoping someone will remember something that can help us. I know it's a long shot. Es-pecially twenty years later."

"We don't have anything to lose," Daniel stated.

The next morning, Lanier hummed softly as she headed to her office, waving in greeting to members of the police officers and detectives. Her first stop was the break room for coffee. She wasn't in the mood for herbal tea. She needed something stronger. She glimpsed a box of doughnuts.

"Go on…you know you want one," one of the police officers said.

"I think I will," she responded with a chuckle.

Lanier chose a chocolate glazed doughnut, then turned around to find Daniel behind her. She awarded him a smile. "Good morning." His sensitivity concern-ing her mother's birthday had touched Lanier deeply. There was a part of her that wanted to share the truth about Gayle Giraud, but she couldn't risk it. She didn't want to be taken off the investigation.

He responded in kind. "Did you happen to see if there were any plain ones left?"

"A couple."

Lanier navigated over to the Keurig and slipped in a coffee pod. She bit into the doughnut while waiting for her coffee.

Coffee and doughnut in hand, Lanier entered her office to find that another six boxes had been placed beside her desk. She sat down and finished her *breakfast* before opening the box at the top of the stack.

A call came in about a missing college student, but the alert was canceled an hour later, much to Lanier's relief. She couldn't handle another loss right now.

Not today.

Sure, Lanier experienced moments when her job became overwhelming, but she refused to walk away. She had to see this through—she'd made a promise and she wasn't about to break it.

Chapter Nine

The week passed by quickly. Friday was here before Daniel fully realized it. "I hope you're not planning to be locked up in your suite working the entire weekend," he told Lanier at the end of the workday. He was concerned that she wasn't taking any breaks from the investigation. It was demanding, but they needed some time away to gain fresh insight.

He was relieved when she responded, "I'm coming in for a few hours on Saturday. My best friend is here for a conference. I haven't been able to see her because of her schedule and the investigation. However, we're going to spend a few hours together on Sunday before I take her to the airport."

Daniel broke into a grin. "I'm glad to hear it."

"What about you? Do you have any special plans?" Lanier asked. "I know Michael's on call this weekend."

"On Sunday I plan to attend church and then spend the rest of my day on the couch to catch a game or two. I don't know about you, but my weekends seem to be over before they start."

"You're right about that," Lanier agreed, slipping her tote on her shoulder. "See you on Monday."

"You be careful."

She smiled. "I will, *Dad*."

Daniel held her gaze, liking that smile and wanting to kiss her.

He shook the idea out of his head. It was too easy to get lost in her eyes.

Suddenly the thought of going home to an empty house didn't appeal to Daniel. He picked up the phone and called his mother. "Hey, you want some company?"

Sunday afternoon, Lanier and Celine enjoyed an appetizer tray of cold smoked salmon, cream cheese, minced red onion and capers at Chez Louie while they waited for their entrées to arrive. She was thrilled to see her best friend—she would've enjoyed spending more time with her, but they'd both had a busy week.

"The salmon is delicious," Celine said. "I can't wait to try the chicken and sausage jambalaya."

"Michael told me about this place. I'm looking forward to the crawfish étouffée. He said it's the best in the city."

"Who is Michael?"

"A man with children," Lanier stated. "He and Daniel are partners. We're all working together."

She noted that the ice in the water pitcher was nearly melted as she reached for it. "Ask the server for more ice when you see him."

Celine waved her hand to get the young man's attention. "Could you bring more ice for the water please?" she asked when he approached their table.

He smiled and gave a slight nod. "I'll bring you a fresh pitcher of iced water."

"Thank you so much," she responded, grinning.

Lanier shook her head. "You're such a flirt."

"I just can't help myself," Celine responded. "But you know it's completely harmless. My heart belongs to my boo."

The server returned with more water and a helper carrying a tray with their food.

Lanier waited until they were alone again to speak. "I have a couple of questions for you before you leave." She had met Celine when they were in grad school to get doctorate degrees in forensic psychology. Lanier wanted her input regarding the unsub.

"Lanier. I understand why you're so zealous about these cases. Just remember that it's okay to balance it with other stuff. You should be out here enjoying life."

"I know you're right. I just feel like I can't move forward until I get justice for all those women and my mother."

"Have you gone by the cemetery yet?" Celine asked.

"No, I didn't want to go alone. If you don't mind, can we go by there after brunch so I can put flowers on my mama's and grandmother's graves?"

"I'd be honored to go with you."

"Celine, the FBI tried to recruit you as well. I've always wondered why you chose to be a forensic social worker instead."

"I guess I wanted the best of both worlds," she responded. "I enjoy helping the people the crime affects directly and working with the courts, law enforcement and the criminals."

"You really seem to love your job."

"I do," Celine stated. "Don't you enjoy working for the FBI?"

"It's good, but I think I'd much prefer being a prosecutor or district attorney." Lanier picked up a cracker. "I've been thinking about going to law school once I'm finished with this case."

"Really?"

She nodded. "Yes. Maybe then I can consider having a family. The job I have right now can be a dangerous one."

"There are other positions within the FBI that you are more than qualified for."

"I know, but I'm really leaning toward law school."

"Well, good for you, Lanier. Now tell me about these two detectives you're working with. Are they handsome?"

"Michael isn't bad looking at all—just not my type. You'd like him, though. He's bald, muscular...the only thing is, he's a single father. I'm not sure if he and his wife are divorced yet, but right now they aren't together."

"And the other one?"

"Daniel is gorgeous. He's a man of faith. No wife or children. I don't think he's dating anybody, but I don't know for sure."

"Why haven't you snatched him up, Lanier? I'm sitting here watching you and there's a certain light that shines in your eyes whenever you mention his name."

Lanier dismissed Celine's words with a wave of her hand. "Like I told you before—I don't have time to even think about finding love. This investigation takes priority over everything right now, including romance."

Besides, there was no point in thinking about something that wasn't meant to be.

* * *

Lanier turned into the parking lot of the Sanctuary Park Memorial Cemetery in Kenner. They were greeted by decorative ironwork and sun-bleached aboveground tombs. "The last time I was here was when Nana was buried."

She and Celine stepped out of the rental, locking the doors behind them.

"Wow, these crypts look like concrete buildings," Celine murmured. "They even have street signs and addresses."

"People call them the cities of the dead," Lanier stated.

Two bouquets of flowers in hand, Lanier looked over her surroundings, searching for the gravesite.

They walked up a grassy knoll, keeping close to the path. She'd had to call her aunt for the exact location of the graves.

Lanier glanced down at the directions on her phone. "They should be on the left."

"Here they are," Celine said.

She stared at the private mausoleum that held her mother and grandmother. "I used to feel a strong sense of connection to them in this place. I believed angels stood guard over them while they slept."

"I like that. It's a comforting thought."

"That was when I was a child," Lanier stated. "But now I just feel they're cold and unable to rest—especially my mother, since there's been no justice served."

"But that will change, Lanier. I'll wait outside while you have a moment with them."

She nodded, then used the key her aunt had given her when she'd left for New Orleans.

"Make sure the door stays open," Lanier told Celine. "Being in here makes me a bit claustrophobic."

"I'll be right here."

Inside, Lanier cleared her throat, then addressed her mother's and grandmother's coffins. "I'm sorry I haven't come before now, but I couldn't. I had to wait until I was ready." She placed a bouquet on her mother's dust-and cobweb-covered coffin and the other on her grandmother's. "I miss you both so much."

Tears filled her eyes and rolled down her cheeks.

"I came back here to get justice, and I'm not leaving until I do. Aunt June sends her love. She misses y'all, too. We've both had a hard time with the grieving. We had to see a therapist—I think it was mostly for me, but I'm better now. But I won't be whole until the Crescent City Strangler is caught." She swiped at her eyes before adding, "I promise you both that he won't get away this time."

Chapter Ten

Daniel was walking out of the church with the other members and heading toward his truck when someone called his name. He turned around.

"Hello, Sarah." He'd known Sarah for years. She worked as a reporter for the *New Orleans Sentinel* newspaper.

"How are things going with the investigation?" she inquired. "I hope you're getting some strong leads so you can catch this killer. People are scared. Some think the Crescent City Strangler is back."

"We're doing everything we can to keep everyone safe," he responded. "As for the Crescent City Strangler—the department will not confirm or deny until we have solid evidence."

"I understand," she said with a smile. "Just so you know, this is off the record, Daniel."

"Sarah, I've come to learn that when it comes to reporters, nothing is ever really off the record." Daniel knew her to be trustworthy, but he wasn't about to give her any information regarding his investigation.

"I hope you find the monster responsible for these murders," Sarah stated. "People are afraid. I'm glad you caught Joe Adams. I was heartbroken when I heard about that poor woman's death. Such a shame she couldn't escape that abuser."

Daniel eyed her. He knew full well that Sarah wanted information on the murdered women. The police department just wasn't ready to make any statements. "When do you ever take a day off, Sarah?"

"I'm not working. We're just having a friendly conversation." She glanced up at him.

Daniel laughed. "Yeah right."

"I've heard about the pretty FBI agent you're working with. How come you haven't snatched her up?"

"Remember, I bear the scars of what happened the last time. Right now, I need to focus on keeping New Orleans safe, which has me very busy. I don't have time for a relationship."

"Well, one thing I ask of you, Daniel—I want to be the first person to break the story when you catch the murderer of those women, whether it's the Crescent City Strangler or not. Will you at least give me this?"

He smiled. "As you know—my captain has the final say."

"See you later, old friend." She moved toward him for a hug.

Daniel embraced her. "You still have the Taser I gave you?"

"I do, and I know how to use it," she answered. "A girl can't be too careful these days."

"Sadly, that's true," he stated. The thought of a serial killer on the loose didn't sit well with Daniel at all. He was even more determined to find the murderer. He'd meant what he said about keeping the women of New Orleans safe.

"What time does your flight leave?" Lanier asked Celine when they left the cemetery.

"It's around 9:10 this evening."

"Thanks for earlier. I don't think I could've done it alone." She shuddered involuntarily. "I don't like cemeteries." Lanier didn't regret going, but it had been a grim reminder of all that she'd lost.

"Hey…we're family. You know I got you."

"I know I've been really busy all week, but how would you like to spend your final hours in the Big Easy?"

"Do you mind stopping by the mall?"

"Sure. We can do that. There's one not too far from here."

A few minutes later, Lanier pulled into the entrance of the nearby shopping center.

Celine chuckled as she got out of the vehicle. "You're the only friend I have who hates shopping."

"I don't hate it," Lanier responded. "I just don't love it as much as you do."

A man a few yards away caught her attention.

"Daniel, hey." Lanier greeted him with a warm smile.

"Hello," he responded.

She made introductions.

"So, you're the detective Lanier's working with…" Celine said with a huge grin.

"Guilty."

Lanier hoped Daniel didn't think she'd been talking about him. She didn't want him getting the wrong idea.

"I didn't expect to see you at the mall. I never figured you to be a shopper."

"I need some new shoes and a couple of shirts," Daniel said. "I wouldn't be here otherwise."

"Want some help picking them out?" Celine asked. "Lanier has a very good eye when it comes to fashion."

She sent her friend a sharp glare. "I'm sure Daniel can manage on his own."

Celine grinned. "C'mon. I love shopping for men."

"I can use all the help I can get," Daniel responded.

Lanier was relieved that Celine remained on her best behavior while they were with Daniel. She didn't ask him a bunch of personal questions or try setting them up for a date.

He was decisive and knew what he wanted, so they were in and out of the men's store within an hour.

"I appreciate your help, ladies," Daniel said.

Celine nodded. "It was a pleasure meeting you."

He gave one of his dazzling smiles. "And you as well, Celine."

When Celine and Lanier were done with their shopping, they headed to the car.

"Daniel seems very nice." Celine gave her a sidelong glance.

Lanier laughed. "I knew this was coming."

"Well, he is, and he has an eye for you," Celine said. "That man is into you, girl."

Lanier shook her head in dismissal. "We just work together."

"I'm telling you, Daniel is attracted to you."

"Time to change the subject."

"Okay. I know you wanted to ask me some questions. How can I help?"

"You've often said that serial killers have a fantasy of their victim. Do you believe that particular fantasy can change?" Even though Lanier was the expert on this subject, she often asked Celine her opinion. It felt good to bounce ideas off each other, whether personal or professional.

Celine nodded. "They usually have what I call an *ideal* victim. This is usually based on race, gender and physical characteristics, or it could be another specific quality about him or her. Depending on the killer's environment, the fantasy can change or evolve."

"But it's nearly impossible to find people who meet the exact traits," Lanier stated.

"It's rare. That's why they look for people with similar qualities."

"Which is why they often seem to be completely random at first…" Lanier looked at Celine. "The women in the past were either strippers or prostitutes, and they frequented bars in Tremé and Algiers. My mother worked in a bar. The connection there is obvious. But these recent murders are different."

"You're going to have to look deeper. Each of those women has something in common that only the killer knows about. You have to find out what it is."

After dropping Celine off at the airport later, Lanier returned to the hotel, where she settled on the sofa under a plush throw blanket with a cup of honey and chamomile tea. She remained there relaxing until the bed called for her and sleep pulled her into a dream filled with happy memories of her mother and grandmother.

The next morning, Lanier stopped for a café au lait and beignets on her way to the station. She was in her office enjoying her treat when a knock at the door stole her attention. She looked up, her face warming at the sight of Daniel standing there dressed in royal-blue button-down collared shirt and black slacks.

"Hey. I love that color on you," she said, referring to the shirt she'd picked out for him.

"Thanks. I like it, too. It's a perfect match to the tie your friend chose."

"Celine has great taste."

"Did you two have a nice visit?"

Lanier grinned. "We did."

Their eyes met and held for a moment.

She was the first one to pull her gaze away.

Whenever Lanier was around Daniel, her heart pounded so hard she thought he must certainly be able to hear it, and she needed every bit of concentration to keep her features and her body language evenly composed. Each moment of nearness, Lanier could feel the heat of him, and a small part of her desired to curl against Daniel, soaking up the warmth like a heated blanket in cold weather. For various reasons there was a bond between them, fragile and tenuous, but it was there. Lanier simply chose to ignore it.

It was getting harder to disregard her emotions where Daniel was concerned, but Lanier couldn't afford to let them reign over her life. She needed to place her complete attention on the investigation. She and Daniel enjoyed each other's company, but they were careful about letting the relationship go any further than that.

Lanier couldn't deny her attraction to Daniel was a struggle for her personally. But she'd learned a long time ago how to mask her feelings—to bury them deep within, lest they threaten to consume her.

Clearing her throat softly, Lanier said, "Celine is a

forensic social worker, so I spoke to her regarding a possible link between the recent murders."

Daniel looked relaxed and rested as he sat in the chair across from her desk with his legs crossed.

"What did she have to say?"

"Pretty much what we already know," Lanier responded. "But she said we need to focus most on the reason why the unsub chose his recent victims."

She returned her attention to her monitor, then checked her watch. It was almost time to join a video conference with her team in Virginia.

Five minutes later, Lanier was updating them on the status of the investigation.

The virtual meeting lasted a little over an hour. She ended the conversation by saying, "I'll email my notes to you."

Afterward, she and Daniel made phone calls.

"I don't know about you, but I'm not having much success," Lanier said after her third call. "So far all the family members close to the victims are gone. One is in a nursing home and has dementia."

"There's no one I can contact for Gayle Giraud," Daniel responded. "Her mother died not too long after her death."

"Just move on to the next person," she said. "It's been a long time, but I felt we had to at least try."

Around four o'clock, Daniel said, "Since we're working late, what would you like to eat? My treat."

"I haven't tried a po' boy yet."

Smiling, he said, "I know just the place. I'll place an order for pickup."

"Make mine shrimp, dressed please."

Twenty minutes later, they sat in her office eating their sandwiches.

Lanier met Daniel's intense gaze with a smile. "Thanks for dinner."

He took a long sip of his iced tea.

"This sandwich is everything," she said. "I think I'm addicted to them now."

They made small talk while finishing up their food, and then afterward, it was back to work.

Going through the murder book of Gayle Giraud, Lanier uttered, "I really can't comprehend why a God who is supposed to be so loving punishes good people. I've always heard He allows things to happen for a reason. But I have trouble understanding why." She'd always blamed God for taking her mother away from her. He could've saved her that night but didn't. Over the years, her anger abated, but disappointment remained.

"God is not the cause of human suffering—the enemy is the one responsible. The reality is that people are often victimized by imperfect humans under the power of evil."

"So you don't believe that some people are born evil?"

"I don't," Daniel replied. "I believe that people aren't completely *good*, and because we have been tainted and infected with sin, some people choose to give in to evil."

"I disagree with you." She stared down at the crime scene photos of her mother. "If God cared—He'd do something to right this wrong or he never would've let it happen in the first place."

"He cares, Lanier. Let's talk about Job in the Bible. He was a righteous man, yet he suffered terribly. God allowed Satan to do everything he wanted to Job except kill him, and Satan did his worst. Job didn't understand why God allowed the things He did. However, Job continued to trust in God. I believe this is the desired reaction He wants from us as well."

"I see that you really believe this, but it's still hard for me to comprehend." She laid the folder down on her desk. "Let's just agree to disagree on this subject." Lanier didn't want to challenge his beliefs, and she didn't want him trying to convince her of something she'd never understand. It was another reason why a relationship with him could never progress beyond friendship.

Chapter Eleven

Daniel tugged at his tie and prayed for the strength to stay focused on the task at hand. It was challenging to keep his mind off Lanier. More than once, he'd told himself that she was a distraction he could not afford. The investigation had them bound by an invisible thread, pulling them closer together. He never anticipated it would be this hard to work so closely with a woman like Lanier.

It had been a long day for them both, and they were still at it in her suite. Going through all the cases was time-consuming, but they had to be thorough. Lanier was focused and dedicated. She worked as hard and had logged just as many—or more—hours on this investigation without complaining.

She stretched and yawned, prompting him to say, "If you keep doing that, I'm going to start."

"I'm so sorry," Lanier murmured with a short laugh.

"Why don't we call it a night?" he suggested. "We've been at this for hours."

"I'm good," she responded. "I just need a cup of coffee to boost my energy, and then I'll be ready for the next stack of files."

Stifling a yawn, Daniel uttered, "I can use some myself. Where's the coffee maker?"

"Behind the bar," Lanier said without looking up from the thick notebook on her lap.

He rose to his feet and strode over to the Keurig.

When Daniel returned to the sofa with two cups of coffee, he found Lanier sleeping, a peaceful look on her face.

Smiling, he set them down on the counter, listened until her breathing became steady and deep, then placed a blanket over her before quietly leaving the suite.

Tired and longing for sleep, he made his way to the elevators, taking one down to the lobby.

Daniel headed out to his truck to make the short drive home. His body yearned for a shower to wash away the day. Exhaustion made his eyelids heavy. He was more than ready for bed and a good night's sleep.

After locking up the house, Daniel retired to his bedroom upstairs. He showered, slipped on pajama pants and settled in the middle of his bed to reflect. Although he was sleepy, Daniel retrieved the Bible off his nightstand and read a passage of scripture. After the shooting, he'd committed to having a more intimate relationship with, and deepening his devotion to, the Lord. Before then, his faith had been nothing more than lip service. Now it was a part of his lifestyle.

He prayed, then decided to turn in for the night.

Daniel rested his head on his pillow, hoping for sleep to come. He hadn't been able to rest well since the first new murder. Sleep did not come easily because every time he closed his eyes, he saw the faces of the victims—the women whose lives were cut short by an unknown, ruthless killer.

Lanier's sleep was interrupted by a call from Daniel. When she answered, he said, "Hey, I'm at the hospital. A woman was assaulted earlier. I've requested that we take over the case. You should come to the hospital."

"I'm on the way," she responded, sitting up in bed. If Daniel had called her, then the incident had something to do with the unsub. They didn't talk long, so Lanier had no idea of the severity of the victim's injuries. No one had ever come forward; it was just assumed there were no living witnesses.

Lanier rushed to her feet and slipped on a pair of black pants, a black turtleneck and boots. She grabbed her leather jacket and tote.

Fifteen minutes later, Lanier met Daniel and Michael at the hospital.

"The victim is Abra Spence," Daniel said. "She was hysterical when they brought her here, but she's quieted down since. The doctor's examining her right now."

"What happened?"

"She was almost strangled," Michael said.

He had her full attention. Lanier twisted her hair into a bun and stuck in a couple of hairpins to secure it. "With a garrote?"

Daniel nodded.

Lanier glanced over her shoulder when the doctor walked out of the room. "I'm going to see what I can find out from the victim. What's her name again and has a family member been notified?" she asked Daniel.

"Abra Spence," he responded. "Her husband is in Cincinnati on business. He's flying home tomorrow morning."

Lanier knocked softly before opening the door and stepping inside. "Hello, Mrs. Spence. I'm Special Agent Lanier Barrow with the FBI."

"C'mon in…" she mumbled.

She entered alone, leaving Daniel and Michael in the hall, and quickly assessed the woman in the bed. Lanier could see tears pressed against Abra's eyes that were threatening to escape. She knew the young woman was struggling not to break down. Not here. Not in front of people she didn't even know. There was a quiet strength about Abra, which meant she prided herself on keeping her composure, especially now. She didn't want to be looked upon as a victim. There was evidence that she'd fought back, which showed courage and determination to escape her attacker. Lanier admired these qualities because she felt the same way. She would never allow anyone to have that kind of power over her. In this instance, she and Abra were kindred spirits.

Her eyes traveled to the woman's left hand. Abra's wedding band was still in place.

She navigated closer to the bed and asked, "Do you feel up to telling me what happened?"

Abra gave a tense nod of consent. "The guy didn't know who he was messing with." She lifted her chin in defiance. "I was in the army. I'm a *vet*. I was at the Nouveau Lounge with a friend. Since it wasn't far from my house, I decided to walk home. I live on Marais Street, three blocks from the bar."

Lanier nodded. "What time was it when you left the bar?"

"About 2:30 in the morning. I was only a block away

from my home." She paused a moment, then continued. "Somebody grabbed me from behind, but I was able to break his hold and flip him."

"Were you able to get a look at his face?" Lanier asked, suddenly hopeful. If this woman had seen her attacker, they might finally have their murderer.

"Naw…he had on this black hoodie, some kinda black covering on his face, black gloves… I can't tell you if he was black, white…nothing." Her eyes conveyed the fury within her, and Lanier's stomach sank. "All I know is that once I was free, I jumped on him and started punching. The whole time I was screaming and screaming and screaming. He managed to knock me off him, and he ran away."

"It was your screams that woke up your neighbors," Lanier informed her. "A couple of them called 9-1-1."

"I heard footsteps behind me, but I thought it was my friend." Abra shook her head, breaking her composure. Angry tears streamed down her face. "He kept trying to put this thick rope thing around my neck… I knocked it out of his hand, and I kept fighting harder and screaming."

Lanier eyed the bruising around Abra's neck. "You were very brave."

Her nostrils flaring with anger, she said, "The *one night* I didn't have my Taser with me."

"Can you tell me anything about his height?"

"He was over six feet tall, I think. I just know he was dressed in all black. I wish I could've ripped that mask— whatever it was—off his face." Abra spat out the words contemptuously before breaking down into sobs. "I was so scared, but then I just got angry. I figured if I had to die, I was gonna try my best to take him with me."

Lanier embraced her. "You're safe now."

A nurse entered the room, and Abra asked for something to help her sleep. "I don't want to relive this nightmare," she said. "I want my husband."

Lanier smiled gently. "He should be here when you wake up in the morning."

"I can't believe it. I was almost murdered... I was targeted by that serial killer that's been killing those women." Her eyes were suddenly filled with fear. "What if he tries to come here?"

Lanier shook her head. "A police officer will be posted outside your door."

"There's been talk around town that the Crescent City Strangler might be back." Abra shuddered involuntarily. "I hope that's not true."

It unsettled Lanier that the community knew he was back. But then, this community had lived through this nightmare before.

The drug Abra was given began to take effect. She closed her eyes, then slowly opened them again.

"You've had quite a night, so I'll let you get some rest."

"Please don't leave yet," Abra said.

"I'll wait until you fall asleep."

Lanier sat down in the chair near the window. It thrilled her that Abra had survived her attack, and she hoped this failed attempt on her life would bring them closer to finding the unsub.

Daniel and Michael remained outside the hospital room while Lanier talked to Abra inside.

Leaning against the wall, Daniel said, "She has bruising around her neck. The officer told me she put up a good fight, though."

Michael gave a short sigh. "Looks like Abra Spence was almost the fifth victim…it's been a while since the last victim. I was hoping there would be no more vics."

"The Lord was looking out for Mrs. Spence." Just as the words left Daniel's mouth, he noticed a man standing at the other end of the corridor at the nurse's station.

Their gazes met for a moment before the man made a sudden turn to leave.

"Hey," Daniel called out.

The man broke into a sprint down the hallway.

Daniel ran after him, prompting Michael to join the chase. The guy practically dived into an open elevator and was gone by the time they got there. They ran to the nearest stairway and rushed down to the lobby.

"He must have gotten off on one of the other floors," Michael said between breaths.

Daniel stopped at a nearby nurse's station and requested that security shut down the hospital. Breathing hard, he wiped away beads of perspiration on his forehead. He hoped the guy hadn't escaped.

There were several men in the hospital fitting the description: black hoodie and jeans. A couple were of the same general height, but after speaking with them, he ruled them out as the person they were chasing.

After a thorough search of the hospital, Daniel surmised that the man had managed to evade them. His hand clenched into a fist. "I can't believe he was able to get away that quickly." He continued to scan the immediate area.

"I'll go check in with Lanier."

He went to room 404 and knocked softly.

Lanier came to the door, and Daniel motioned for her to join him in the hallway.

"Did something happen out here?" She kept her voice just above a whisper.

"We spotted some guy at the nurse's station earlier dressed in black from head to toe, hiding his face with a hoodie. When he saw me, he took off and ran. Michael's talking to security about viewing the camera footage. We're going to need a subpoena, so we won't be able to get a hold of it until tomorrow morning." Daniel gave a slight nod toward the door. "How is Mrs. Spence doing?"

"As you can imagine, she's very shaken and afraid," Lanier responded. "The nurse gave her a sedative to help her sleep. They want to keep her overnight."

Daniel nodded. "I spoke to the nurse that the dude was talking to—he was asking about Abra."

"Abra mentioned that she'd met a friend at the bar. However, she referred to the friend as *she*," Lanier stated. "I don't think a friend would just take off running like that. Does he fit the profile for the unsub?"

"Yeah, he did, but I don't think he's bold enough to show up in a place like this. Nonetheless, I've requested that a policeman be posted outside her door. Did she happen to give you any information about the friend she was with?"

"No," Lanier responded. "But I'll make sure to ask Abra when I come back later this morning."

He rubbed his left eye with his hand. "I'm sorry to ruin your Saturday night like this."

"It's fine," she said, then stifled a yawn. "I'm going back to the hotel to get some sleep, and then I'll come back here in a few hours."

"I'll walk out with you," Daniel said.

Lanier paused in her tracks. "Michael, you should leave, too. You should be home when your children wake up."

He rubbed his eyes. "Pretty soon my babysitter will be moving in, at the rate I've needed her lately."

"We've been pulling some long hours," Daniel agreed.

Michael stretched and yawned. "I'm outta here."

Daniel nodded. "Lanier and I will be right behind you."

After Michael left, Daniel said, "After you talk to Abra, we'll go by security to view the surveillance video. I'm requesting the subpoena first thing."

She released another yawn. "Okay. I need to get some sleep. I can hardly think straight right now."

"I'll walk you to your car," he offered again.

Lanier didn't argue with Daniel. Instead, she followed him quietly to the parking lot. He made sure she was safe inside her rental and on her way to the hotel before driving in the opposite direction.

Daniel glanced at the clock. It was almost five thirty. He had to be at the court as soon as it opened, then back at the hospital.

It was going to be a long day.

Chapter Twelve

Lanier protested loudly when her alarm released a steady, annoying ringtone at eight o'clock. She eased out of bed and padded barefoot across the floor to the bathroom. She shivered a little when her feet touched the cold ceramic tile.

She showered quickly and dressed in a suit.

Exactly one hour later, Lanier walked out of the hotel to her vehicle and was soon on her way back to the hospital, fueled by three and a half hours of sleep.

Lanier was seated beside Abra's bed, sipping a cup of coffee, when she woke up.

"You're back," she uttered as she sat up slowly, wincing and gingerly touching her neck.

"I have a few more questions for you, Mrs. Spence," Lanier stated. "I hope you were able to rest well."

Abra cleared her throat. "I've already told you everything I remember."

"You told the police officer that you were out with a friend. We didn't have a chance to talk about this friend. Can you give me a name?"

She looked away, then shifted restlessly in bed. "Why

you need to know her name? She don't have nothing to do with what happened to me."

Lanier offered a sympathetic look, hoping the woman might open up. "I'm curious as to why your friend didn't come looking for you. Did you go to the bar together, or did you meet her there? And why didn't she hear you screaming?"

She shrugged. "I met up with her there. The music in that bar is loud, Agent Barrow," Abra muttered. "I doubt if anyone inside heard me. Plus, I was two blocks away."

Lanier glanced down at her notes. "Do you normally walk home whenever you go out?"

"I've done it a few times," Abra stated. "I don't understand why you're asking me about all this instead of trying to find the attacker. I've been through enough, and I just want to go *home*."

"I may need to speak with your friend. She may have noticed someone in the bar who fits the description of your attacker."

"I was all over that bar, and I didn't see anyone that looked strange or scary," Abra said.

"Is this a place you frequent?"

"Not really. I just go there to see my friend."

"This friend of yours…male or female?" Lanier pressed once more.

"I said *she* earlier. *What*? You don't believe me?"

Lanier shook her head, gently saying, "I'm not trying to upset you—just trying to get information that may lead us to your attacker."

"My friend wasn't there when I was attacked so she didn't see anything, *okay*? Lady, you focusing on the wrong thing. *I was attacked.* Y'all need to find that killer."

Lanier regarded her. The woman seemed more agitated this morning—though Lanier couldn't blame her. "I was told they're releasing you today."

"Yes. I'm going to spend some time with my mama in Florida. This happened too close to my house. I'm not ready to stay there…you know."

"What about your husband? Will he be joining you?"

"For a week or two, then he's gonna come home," Abra said. "Right now, I don't know when I'll be back. I hope you find that murderer soon."

"We're working hard to get your assailant off the streets," Lanier assured her. With a few parting remarks a short while later, Lanier left the room.

Daniel was in the waiting area when she walked out of the hospital room. She sat down beside him. "I asked Abra about her friend. She became very defensive. She kept saying she doesn't want this friend involved. She's scared, though. Abra's going to stay in Florida with her mother for a while."

A man approached them. "A nurse told me y'all are police detectives. Can you tell me what happened to my wife? I received a call from someone here at the hospital. All they said was that she was attacked."

Daniel briefed him on what had happened.

"Your wife is quite a fighter," Lanier said. "She was able to fend off her attacker."

"Yes, she is," he responded. "I'd like to see Abra."

"She's in that room," Daniel replied as he pointed to her room a few feet away.

"Lanier, what are you thinking?" he asked when they were alone. "I recognize that look on your face."

Initially, she was a bit taken aback by his comment. *Did Daniel really know her that well*? "I keep thinking about the man we're looking for. Maybe he's the *friend* she was with that night—maybe he's a little more than a friend. Did anyone check to see if there were any cameras inside the bar?"

"There aren't," Daniel responded. "Not even outside."

"Did you get the subpoena for the video surveillance?"

He nodded. "Michael's already with hospital security. I told him we'd meet him there."

Lanier tossed the empty coffee cup into a nearby trash can. "Lead the way…"

Daniel, Lanier and Michael reviewed the surveillance cameras at the hospital on the second floor.

"That's the guy right there. The one dressed in all black." Michael pointed to the monitor.

Lanier stared at the man on the screen, trying to memorize his facial features.

He leaned in closer. "He looks familiar to me… Daniel, that's the dude that ran track for LSU a few years ago. Remember, he nearly made it to the Olympics." Michael moved out of the way so Daniel could get a better look.

"You think that's Marcus LaSalle?"

"That's him," Michael insisted. "I'm sure of it."

Daniel checked his watch. "Let's see if we can find Mr. LaSalle and have a conversation with him."

"I'm going to the station," Lanier told them.

"You don't want to talk to him?" Michael asked. "He could be the perp we've been looking for."

"I don't think so," she responded. "My gut tells me this is something else entirely."

He wore a confused expression. "You don't believe she was attacked?"

"Oh, I do, and I suspect it was the unsub, but this man is someone else. He may be a witness at best."

"I guess we'll see where he fits in this puzzle," Daniel said. "He's connected to Abra in some way. We just need to find out how."

"Why don't we bring her in to see if she can identify him?" Michael suggested.

"I don't trust that Abra will be honest, especially since her husband is with her now," Lanier responded.

"You're thinking she and Marcus are involved."

"It's a strong possibility."

"I guess we'll find out." Michael opened the door and they walked toward the exit.

Daniel and his partner caught up with Marcus just as he was leaving his apartment. He looked as if he was about to take off running again, but then decided against it.

"I ain't do nothing."

"Why did you run away?" Daniel asked. He was careful with his tone, to not come off as confrontational. Marcus already looked cagey and distrusting.

"I don't mess around with the *police*," he said with a slight look of defiance.

"We'd like you to come down to the station with us," Michael said. "We just want to talk to you."

Shaking his head, Marcus uttered, "Y'all looking for someone to blame those murders on. The only thing I'm guilty of is messing around with a married woman."

Daniel glanced over at Michael, then back at Marcus. "Look, we have questions, and you may possibly have some if not all of the answers. Come to the station with us."

"How is Abra?"

"She's fine. We can discuss all this once we get to the station," Daniel stated.

"Why can't we just talk here?"

"You're not under arrest," Michael said. "We just have questions."

Marcus swallowed hard, then lifted his chin, saying, "It's not like I really have a choice."

Sullen, he got into the back seat of the car. He didn't utter a word the entire ride to the station.

Michael and Daniel both joined him in the interrogation room.

"What do you know about the recent murders of several women?" Daniel asked.

Marcus held his hands up in resignation. "I don't know nothing about them outside of what's been said on the news. I don't read the paper. Hey, y'all ain't gon' blame this on me."

Michael asked, "How do you know Abra Spence?"

"We met on this dating site."

"Are you the friend she was with on the night of her attack?" Daniel questioned.

"Yeah. We met at Nouveau Lounge."

"What happened the night Abra was attacked?"

"We got into an argument over something stupid, and she decided to leave."

"You didn't go after her?" Michael asked.

"Ain't no talking to that woman when she mad. I figured she'd go outside and cool off, then come back. When I walked outside after the bar closed, all I saw was an ambulance and police cars. I didn't know it was Abra until one of the bartenders told me. She and Abra are friends."

"Can someone confirm that you never left the bar that night until closing?"

"The bartender I mentioned earlier. Her name is Ebony. I don't know her last name. She's Abra's friend."

"Abra is cheating on her husband," Lanier stated at the police station. "I have to say I'm a bit surprised she's bold enough to do it three blocks from her home."

"Doesn't sound as if her husband is home much—maybe Abra wants to rub it in his face," Daniel suggested.

"I feel like we're not getting anywhere with this case," Lanier uttered in frustration. "This guy is always a few steps ahead of us. Every time a woman is attacked, I feel responsible—like I'm not doing my job. *We've got to find the unsub.*" She was exhausted from the long hours working, and it irked her that they hadn't gotten a strong lead. "We're not getting anywhere."

"It's not your fault, Lanier," Daniel said. "I'm nowhere near giving up. The people of my beloved city will not live in fear. We're going to find him."

Lanier wanted to find a way to draw the murderer out, but the last time she tried it, she'd ended up in the hospital.

This time I'll be smarter.

She decided not to mention it to Daniel. She didn't need his protection. His presence could hinder her progress, especially if the attacker was looking for women alone. Her goal was to canvass a few more bars and see if the unsub would try once more to come after her.

Her first stop would be the Nouveau Lounge. Maybe the unsub was a steady patron. It was possible nothing would come of this, but Lanier had to try. She had to do it for the women who had died, and for his potential next victims.

Chapter Thirteen

Lanier put on a dress that clung to her, her gun strapped to her thigh and another one in her purse. She sauntered through the door of the Nouveau Lounge and slowly made her way to the bar.

A man of average height got up, allowing her to take his seat. His description didn't fit that of Abra's attacker. "Thanks," she uttered.

"I haven't seen you around here before," a young woman said from behind the bar. She wore honey-blond braids that reached past her waist, and her smooth mocha complexion was free of makeup.

"This is my first time here, Ebony."

The woman appeared taken aback. "How do you know my name?" she asked above the music pulsing around them.

Lanier pointed to her name badge. "You seem to have a great memory for faces."

"I do. I'm pretty good with names, too."

"I'm Lanier."

"What would you like to drink?"

"Seltzer or tonic water with lime."

"Not a drinker, I see," Ebony said, leaning in. "You must be that FBI agent Abra told me about. She said you had some questions for me. I was in here working and didn't see anything, but I'll do what I can to help."

"Are you able to take a break?"

"Sure. I own this place." She gestured for one of her employees to take care of the customers in her absence.

"How long have you known Abra Spence?" Lanier asked when she followed Ebony into a small office behind the bar.

"Since we were kids. We used to live across the street from each other. I would babysit her from time to time. I'm actually five years older than Abra, so she's like a little sister to me."

"Abra told me she was at this bar with a friend. Was she referring to you?"

"Look, I already know Marcus was picked up by the police and questioned, so y'all already know the deal on that. She would come to talk, and sometimes they met up here. The thing is, my friend was attacked. Don't you think y'all should be more focused on who tried to kill her instead of worrying about her personal life?"

"This is exactly what I'm doing," Lanier said. "That's why I'm here, Ebony. I don't care about Abra's infidelity. But I do want to know if you noticed anyone in here that night that wasn't a regular."

"I don't get many tourists," Ebony responded. "Just people from the neighborhood mainly come here. It's rare to see a new face. When we do, it's a cop usually." She gave Lanier a pointed look.

"What about tonight?" Lanier asked.

"Outside of you, there have been a couple of new faces in here tonight. There's a dude in a black shirt.

He's one of them pretty boys with good hair. He's sitting at the end of the bar—at least he was before we came in here. I haven't seen him here before."

"One more question," Lanier said. "Does Abra's husband know about her affair?"

"He suspects something. That's why Abra and Marcus were arguing the night she got attacked. She wanted to break it off with him."

"Marcus never left to go after her?"

Ebony shook her head. "He sat right here at the bar talking to me. He kept asking me to talk to her because he loved her. Kept saying he wanted to be with Abra."

Lanier nodded. Her gut told her there was something still to learn here, maybe with the other newcomer at the bar. "I think I might hang out here for a while if you don't mind."

"As long as you're looking for a killer, I don't care. Until he's caught, I don't feel comfortable, and I know my employees feel the same way. I make sure security escorts us to our cars."

"You may want to consider installing cameras as well."

"They're being installed on Monday morning." Rising to her feet, Ebony said, "I need to get back out there."

Lanier stopped at the ladies' room before navigating through the sea of people.

Back at the bar, she spotted the man Ebony mentioned, pouring something in a drink. He was soon joined by a young lady dressed in red. When he handed the drink to her, Lanier walked hurriedly in his direction, deliberately bumping into the woman, forcing her to spill the beverage.

"I'm so sorry," Lanier said. "Let me help get this off

the beautiful dress you're wearing. I know how to get it out before it stains."

She took the woman's hand and led her toward the bathroom. On the way, Lanier asked, "What's your name?"

"Rayana."

"I'm Lanier. How well do you know that guy?"

"I just met him. Why? Is he your man?"

"I just watched him put something in your drink while your attention was elsewhere."

"Is that why you bumped into me?"

"Yes."

"Thank you." Shaking her head, she added, "I thought he was a nice guy. This is why I hate coming to places like this. I only came out because my friend talked me into it. Now I just want to go home."

Lanier showed Rayana her badge. "Why don't I walk you to your car?"

Her eyes widened in surprise. "You're FBI?"

"Yes. If you're ready to leave, I'll make sure you do it safely. A word of advice—never leave a drink unattended, and if someone offers to buy you one, make sure you order it and you're the only one who touches it. Even some bartenders can't be trusted."

After making sure Rayana and her friends made it to their car without incident, Lanier headed back inside to talk to the man at the bar.

"Where's my girl?" he asked as she approached.

Lanier looked him in the eye. "I don't think she's your girl, but the young lady you just tried to drug decided to leave."

He looked shocked. "I don't know what you're talking about."

"Did you know that spiking someone's drink is a felony and carries a maximum ten-year prison sentence?"

His eyes instantly grew wide with fear. "I can't go to jail. I just wanted to have some fun. My friend told me that *Special K* would loosen up a girl." He paused a moment, like he was grasping for words, then added, "My wife is pregnant. She's on bed rest and could lose the baby—this would devastate her, and she could go into labor..." He teared up. "I ain't never done nothing like this before. I didn't know it was a crime."

Lanier shook her head in disgust. "You have a wife at home with a high-risk pregnancy, and you're slipping women ketamine?"

He threw his shaking hands up. "I came here to try to relieve some stress."

"Next time, take up boxing or weight-lifting."

"Are you a cop?"

"No, FBI Special Agent Barrow," she said. "I think it's time you go home to your pregnant wife. Best way to stay out of trouble."

"Thank you," he responded.

"Oh, and hand over the Special K."

"I don't have no more. I swear it."

Lanier eyed him, then gave a nod toward the door. "Get out of here."

The next day in her office, Lanier told Daniel what had happened the night before. It frustrated him that she'd gone to a bar alone. It was careless on her part.

"I'm pretty sure you weren't at the Nouveau Lounge for the drinks or music. Lanier, you have to know going rogue like that can get you killed." He couldn't believe she would put herself at risk that way.

"I was very careful," she responded, her vexation evident. "I just couldn't stand by and let that dude spike the young lady's drink."

"I get that, but we have a killer running loose, and he's got you on his radar."

"I realize that, Daniel…but looks like he's lost interest in me. Maybe we were wrong." She sounded almost regretful, but it was a relief to Daniel. She'd already been hurt working this case, and he didn't want it to happen again. "Regardless, these cases are not going to close themselves. We have high-risk jobs—jobs we're trained to do. I need you to have a little faith in my ability to do this job." Lanier looked away without waiting for a reply.

She was right. It wasn't his place to advise her on safety precautions. "My apologies, Lanier," he said.

She eyed him. "Tell me something…are you one of those men who believe women are fragile creatures who need rescuing?"

"Actually, no. I'm protective of *all* the people I care about."

She stared up at Daniel, the words he'd let slip out hanging between them. "I'd do the same for Michael," he added quickly. "What about you? You ran to that young woman's rescue, and you teach self-defense. You empower people. I try to do the same. We're not that different."

She seemed to consider his words. "Thank you for caring about what happens to me. I do appreciate it."

"And I do have faith in your abilities, Lanier," he stated before leaving her office.

His cell phone rang a few minutes after he sat down at his desk. "Happy Birthday, Sarah," he said after accepting the call.

"Thank you. That's the reason for my call. I'd like to celebrate tonight by having dinner with you. Please tell me you're not working late."

Daniel smiled. "I'm actually free this evening. I'd be honored to celebrate with you." He wasn't the type of person to let a friend spend her birthday alone. "What time should I pick you up?"

"I made reservations for seven o'clock at Antoine's."

"You love that place," he said with a chuckle. Anytime they had dinner together, it was usually Antoine's. Daniel couldn't complain. He enjoyed the ambiance and the food as much as Sarah.

"Yes, I do," she responded.

"Sounds like you have a date," Michael stated when he hung up the phone.

"No," Daniel answered. "Just dinner with Sarah. It's her birthday. You know she and I will never be anything other than friends."

"You better be careful with that one," Michael warned. "She will try to weasel out any information she can about this investigation. Next thing you know, it'll be in the newspaper."

"I can handle Sarah. I'm not giving her any information until we're ready to release it to the public."

They laughed. "You really are a good man, Daniel. I'm older, but I look up to you as a role model."

He arched an eyebrow in surprise. "Michael, what's up? You getting emotional on me?"

"No, just saying…" His friend grew quiet suddenly.

"I guess I should clear my desk before I leave. I have to stop off and buy a card for Sarah and one for my mom. Today is my parents' anniversary."

"You not gon' buy a gift for her?" Michael asked. "We are talking about *Sarah*."

Daniel chuckled. "I better at least get her a gift card to her favorite spa. She'd never let me hear the end of it. She bought me a really nice watch for my birthday."

"I remember," Michael said. "She'd like that. Well, I need to get up outta here myself. I have basketball practice tonight." Michael grinned. "I have a really good team this year."

Daniel nodded. "I applaud you for having the patience to work with at-risk teens." He'd always admired that about his partner.

"I keep telling you that you should be my assistant coach. You'd be good at it. Besides, the boys have a lot of respect for you. They appreciate you taking time to come watch them play."

"I don't know… I'll have to think on it." These days, Daniel couldn't focus on much beyond catching their killer.

An hour later, Daniel waved goodbye to Lanier on his way out of the station.

His first stop was the florist to pick up some flowers for his mother for her wedding anniversary. Since his father's death, Daniel had continued the tradition his dad started—buying a dozen red roses. Next, he bought two cards and a gift certificate.

Daniel parked in front of his mother's house.

"Happy anniversary, Mom," he said when she opened the door.

Her face lit up when she saw the flowers. "Oh Daniel, they're beautiful." She sniffed them, inhaling their fragrance.

He embraced her, then presented the card. "I know

Dad's not here, but I'm sure he's thinking of you and how much he loves and misses you."

She teared up. "I miss him, too. I'm just so surprised you remember that he bought me roses every anniversary. You were only ten years old when we lost him."

"Granddad used to buy them for you until I was old enough to pay for them myself," Daniel said. "He told me he did it for Grandma and that it was a Jordan tradition. When God blesses me with a wife, I plan to do the same for her."

"You father would be so proud of you, Daniel."

"Even though I'm a cop? Dad always wanted me to become a pastor like him and Granddad." Daniel still felt a shred of guilt over choosing law enforcement over serving in the church, but he never felt led to get into ministry.

"That's what he wanted, true enough, but your father understood that God might use you in another way," his mother said. "If you weren't called to the pulpit, you shouldn't be up there."

They chatted for a while, and then Daniel prepared to leave. "I promised Sarah that I'd have dinner with her tonight for her birthday, but if you're free this Friday, we can celebrate your thirty-fifth wedding anniversary."

"I'd love that, son," she responded. "Tell Sarah *happy birthday* for me."

"I will," Daniel said. He kissed her on the cheek. "I love you, Mom."

He left and headed home.

Before she left the station, Lanier decided to try a restaurant she'd heard about on television, Antoine's. She didn't relish eating out alone, but she was tired of room service at the hotel.

"I'd like a reservation for tonight at seven," she said when she called and spoke with the hostess.

"What's the name on the reservation?"

"Lanier Barrow."

Once she was in her suite, she rested on the sofa for thirty minutes, then jumped into the shower.

Twenty minutes later, while she was applying her makeup, Lanier was interrupted by a phone call.

"Hey, what are you up to this evening?" Celine asked when she answered.

"I just made reservations for this place called Antoine's. I saw a commercial, and the food looked so good, I figured I'd treat myself to a nice dinner. Then I'm thinking of going to the House of Blues. I need a night out." Lanier thought about the conversation with Daniel about not going out alone.

"You deserve it. You've been working a lot on that investigation. You need to take a break to enjoy yourself. Just be careful."

She planned to, and if getting to know the city's night-life further helped the case, so much the better. "You're absolutely right, and I plan to do just that—enjoy a night out on the town." She hadn't told her aunt or Celine about the hit-and-run. Lanier didn't want them worried about her.

They talked for a few minutes more before ending the conversation.

Lanier decided on an orange dress with black leather boots. She grabbed a black leather car coat and left the hotel. She was looking forward to an evening of good food at the renowned restaurant that was established in 1840 and considered the birthplace of oysters Rockefeller.

She was seated in the main dining room. Photographs of the rich and famous lined the walls of the restaurant. The family-owned facility featured at least fifteen themed rooms for private dining. As she took in the splendor of her surroundings, Lanier saw the last person she expected to see tonight.

Daniel. And he wasn't alone.

Great. I would come to Antoine's on a night he's here with a date.

Lanier was grateful the table where she was seated wasn't anywhere near Daniel's. She hoped he wouldn't spot her. If she'd known he was dining there, she would've gone to another restaurant.

Strangely, her sunny mood dimmed when she saw them, but she tried to dismiss that as nothing but a temporary feeling. The truth was that she had no right to feel anything where Daniel was concerned.

They worked together.

Nothing more.

Still, she couldn't seem to tear her eyes away from the couple. He looked happy. Lanier had assumed Daniel was single—he'd never mentioned a girlfriend—but she could be wrong. They had never talked about their personal relationships.

Lanier thought she'd detected his attraction to her and she to him, but neither of them had crossed that line. She often wondered why Daniel never approached her, but seeing him now with his date—well, she questioned if she'd been wrong about him. She must've misread whatever she thought she saw in his eyes whenever she caught him watching her.

* * *

"Thanks so much for joining me for dinner," Sarah said after the waiter brought their drinks. "I didn't want to celebrate another birthday alone." He hated hearing the note of sadness in his friend's voice. She'd gotten her natural hair flat-ironed, then styled in loose curls—she normally wore it in two-strand twists—and looked pretty in a red pantsuit. He prayed the right man would come along. Sarah deserved to love and be loved.

"You're a beautiful woman, Sarah. I bet next year you'll be here with a date," he said with a wink, hoping to lift her mood.

She met his gaze. "I don't know…"

"Don't…tonight's a celebration."

She smiled. "You've always been there for me." Laying the menu down, she said, "I will never forget the day you went after those boys who stole my very first cell phone. I was so afraid my parents would be upset with me. I don't know how you did it, but you got it back."

Daniel laughed at the memory. "I followed that boy all the way home and jumped him. When his mother came out of the house, I told her what he'd done. She made him give it to me."

"You are such a wonderful and caring person," Sarah murmured. "I just wish you'd open your heart and let someone love you."

He shook his head. "Let's not go there. With this investigation, there isn't room for romance in my busy schedule."

"Even if there were no murders—no investigation—you'd still choose your work. You're married to your job."

"You know I want more than that."

"All you do is work. You actually have to get out more to meet someone." She glanced around the dining room, then asked, "Daniel, did you by chance mention at work that you were dining here this evening?"

"No, why do you ask?"

"Isn't that the FBI agent you've been working with sitting over there?"

He glanced over to his left, astonished to see Lanier. "Yes, that's her." She'd mentioned how much she hated eating in public alone. Maybe she was meeting someone here.

"I've known you a very long time," Sarah stated, interrupting his thoughts. "Agent Barrow is very special to you. I can see it in your eyes. They just lit up like fireworks."

He didn't respond. It was true that he was falling for Lanier, but it wasn't something he was ready to give voice to or discuss with his friend. Daniel hadn't fully grasped the weight of his feelings. He'd never felt anything like what he felt for her.

"She's gorgeous and *alone*," Sarah said. "Why don't you invite her to join us?"

"She could be waiting for her date to arrive."

"Daniel, do you really believe that? *A woman who looks like her?* She'd wait for no man. Now go over there and ask her to join us."

"You don't mind?"

"No, the more the merrier." Sarah grinned. "It's my birthday."

Daniel pushed away from the table and strode across the room. Lanier looked up from her menu just as he approached. "I didn't expect to see you here."

"I can say the same of you," she responded.

"Why don't you join me and my friend?" he asked. "It's her birthday."

Shaking her head, Lanier stated, "I don't want to intrude…" And she clearly didn't want Daniel asking her to join them out of pity.

"Sarah is like a sister to me," he said. "And she sent me over here to get you. Join us."

"Are you sure?"

"If you don't come with me, Sarah will be over here to get you. It's her birthday," he repeated.

"Okay. Sure." Lanier gave up her table to join Daniel and his friend.

He released a soft sigh of relief. He was glad she'd agreed to have dinner with them. Daniel always enjoyed her company. He also believed she and Sarah would get along well.

Daniel tried to ignore how beautiful Lanier looked. He told himself his reason for wanting her with him was for her protection. At least he could make sure she returned to the hotel safely tonight.

Deep down, he knew it was much more than that, but he wasn't ready to admit it—not even to himself.

Chapter Fourteen

"Thank you for allowing me to join you," Lanier said as she sat down in the chair Daniel held out for her. "Happy birthday." She was grateful not to have to eat alone.

He quickly made introductions.

"It's so nice to finally meet you, Lanier," Sarah stated. "From what I've heard, you have an impressive career."

"Sarah is a reporter," Daniel said. "But she's promised to be on her best behavior tonight. We are going to enjoy our meal and celebrate my dear friend."

Sarah laughed. "He's right. I promise tonight is all about fun. After we eat, we should go dancing."

"I was planning to go to House of Blues," Lanier said. "Why don't you two join me?"

"That's the place I had in mind," Sarah responded. "This is turning out to be a wonderful birthday celebration. We're gonna have such a great time."

"What do you think of New Orleans, Lanier?" Sarah asked while they were waiting for their food to arrive.

"I love it here. I wish I had more time to enjoy the city."

"Daniel's a workaholic, so you're gonna have to—"

"I'm not the only reason," he quickly interjected. "We're pulling all these hours because of her."

"He's right," Lanier said. "Daniel and I have that in common. We're both workaholics. Enough about work. We're here to celebrate you."

Sarah laughed. "Yes, this *is* all about me."

Lanier liked her. She enjoyed the light bantering back and forth between Sarah and Daniel. She could tell they were close.

"I can't wait to get out on the dance floor." Sarah glanced at Daniel, then said, "Lanier, I hope you like dancing. This dude here isn't a dancer."

"I was able to get him to dance with me a few times," Lanier responded.

"Whaaat?" Sarah looked completely shocked.

"It was while we were canvassing a spot for the case," Daniel admitted. He took a sip of his iced tea, then said, "I didn't do that great a job."

Laughing, Lanier nodded. "But he tried."

"You were able to get him to do something I never could." Sarah gave Daniel a mischievous look. "I really like you, Lanier."

The waiter arrived with their meals.

"Everything looks delicious," Lanier murmured, looking down at the food before her.

Sarah agreed. "The food here is divine. Just enjoy."

Lanier couldn't remember the last time she'd laughed so hard. Daniel's friend was witty and charming. She had a great time as they ate and chatted through the meal.

While they were waiting for dessert to arrive, Sarah asked, "Are you a single gal like me?"

Lanier took a sip of water, then smiled. "I am."

"I'll have to invite you to some of our single girl out-ings."

Lanier glanced briefly at Daniel before saying, "I'd like that." It might do her some good to get to know people outside of the police station. She needed a life outside of her work, and tonight reminded her of that. She was realizing this more and more as necessary for her mental health. She promised herself that she'd get a better work/life balance—after she caught the Cres-cent City Strangler.

The next day, Lanier sat at a small table enjoying a cup of chai tea and beignets at a café a block away from the station when she overheard two women talking.

"...that Michael Durousseau can arrest me anytime," one of them said. "He is one *fine* detective. And don't forget he's *rich*. Sole heir to the family millions."

The other woman agreed. "And he's such a nice man. I can't believe his wife just up and left him like that, leaving those poor kids behind."

"I know. He's already been through so much—his mother committed suicide when we were in college, and then his dad went missing a couple years later. He took a year off, but he went back to school and com-pleted his degree."

Lanier was astounded by what they were saying. She'd had no idea about the tragedies Michael faced as a young man. Although he was much older when he lost his parents, his grief was probably just as great as what she'd experienced. Lanier admired his fortitude to move past his pain and become a renowned homicide detective while raising his children as a single father.

As soon as Lanier returned to the station, she searched

through articles, curious to learn more about Michael's father, Robert Durousseau. Her interest was piqued when she read that the wealthy businessman disappeared twenty years ago, a day after the body of her mother was found.

Every fiber of her being went on alert. *This isn't a coincidence.*

Lanier couldn't explain why she felt this way. The feeling that Michael's father was a piece of the puzzle intensified the more she thought about it. But was it too convenient?

Was she just reaching for any connections she could find at this point?

I'm overthinking this. Robert Durousseau's disappearance probably has nothing to do with the investigation.

Michael was off, so Lanier could discuss what she'd learned about his partner's family with Daniel. It seemed she and Michael had a lot in common.

Lanier called Daniel into her office. When he entered, she closed the door behind him.

"Earlier when I was out grabbing a bite to eat, I heard two women discussing Michael. They mentioned that he lost his mother to suicide, and his father just disappeared one day and no one has seen him since."

"People like to talk. You know that."

"It's clear that Michael's been through a lot. Yet he works a demanding job and is a single father. I guess it helps to have millions at your disposal."

"That's because he doesn't care about the money," Daniel stated. "Michael donates his salary to a local church to help the homeless. He also volunteers his time at a teen center and coaches a youth basketball team."

"I googled Michael's dad, and I came across an article that said he's been missing twenty years. He disappeared the very next day after Gayle Giraud was found. Don't you find it a bit strange?" Lanier was experiencing a mixture of emotions since learning this information. She cautioned herself to take time to formulate her thoughts. She didn't want to jump to conclusions, but she couldn't deny that Robert's disappearance around the time of her mother's murder brought more questions.

Daniel eyed her. "What are you suggesting, Lanier?"

"Maybe Robert didn't just disappear out of the blue— maybe he's on the run from something."

"I'm sorry, Lanier. From what I heard, Robert abandoned Michael because he couldn't deal with the loss of his wife."

"Who did you hear that from?"

"Michael. The company employees told police that Robert was distraught, and he'd changed after losing his wife. Then one day, he just suddenly disappeared."

"None of that makes it necessarily true," Lanier countered.

"And it doesn't make him guilty either," Daniel stated. "According to Michael, his dad is over in Greece. That's where he's currently living."

She gave him a sidelong glance. "They're in touch, then?"

"Lanier, he's had to deal with a lot. Don't say anything to him about this. Michael told me that he and his father aren't close, but Robert does check in with him— not often, maybe once or twice a year."

Arms folded, she responded, "I just don't think it's a coincidence."

"So you really believe that Robert's disappearance and Gayle Giraud's death are connected?" Daniel asked.

Lanier chewed on her bottom lip. "I don't know... right now I'm just speculating."

"We're exhausted, but we can't go grabbing at straws. *Especially not this straw.* Michael's doing the best he can to be strong for his children. We can't say anything unless we have something tangible."

"Of course," she responded. "I won't say anything to Michael."

But Robert was going to stay on her radar until she had concrete proof he didn't belong there. Lanier didn't believe much in coincidences. She never had and wouldn't start now.

Daniel sat at his desk muddling over the conversation he'd had with Lanier. He didn't quite understand her sudden interest in Robert Durousseau's disappearance.

"Earth to Daniel..."

He glanced up to find Michael standing beside his desk. "Hey, what are you doing here? Don't you have basketball practice or something?" Daniel was surprised to see his partner on his day off.

"I left my keys to the gym here in the drawer. You must have been thinking about something hard. You didn't even hear me approach."

"It wasn't anything important," Daniel responded.

Grinning, Michael asked, "You weren't taking one of those mental staycations or whatever they call it, were you?"

He laughed. "Naw, nothing like that."

Michael peered at Lanier, who was in her office with the door open. "She looks very focused on something. Anything new come up?"

"Nope." Daniel glanced over his shoulder. "You might want to get out of here before Chief sees you. You know he'll try to put you to work."

Michael opened a drawer and pulled out a set of keys. "I'll see you tomorrow, Partner."

"Don't work the team too hard."

"It depends on them." He made his way past several desks toward the exit.

Daniel glanced over his shoulders to find Lanier staring. Their eyes met and held. The air in the station was suddenly charged with a surge of electricity that wrapped around Daniel like a warm blanket.

Chapter Fifteen

Lanier had just drifted off to sleep when the loud ring-ing of the hotel phone jerked her awake. She reached over to answer. "Hello."

"You need to LEAVE New Orleans!" a voice shouted.

Her mood veered sharply to anger. "Who is this?" she demanded. "Man up and tell me who you are!"

"Leave or you'll be sorry." A sudden chill hung on the edge of the man's words.

"I'm not going anywhere," Lanier stated, trying to contain her fury.

The caller hung up.

Fear and anger knotted inside her. Lanier debated whether to call Daniel. It was after midnight, but the call left her unsettled, and she needed to talk it out with someone.

She pulled up his number in her cell and called.

"Hullo…" Daniel sounded like he had been sleeping.

She tried to keep her fragile control. "I'm sorry for waking you up, but I thought you'd want to know about the phone call I just received."

Lanier gave him a recap, her mind fluttering anxiously.

"I'm on my way," Daniel said.

"Okay." She didn't argue or try to talk him out of coming. Lanier didn't want to be alone right now. She hated to admit it, but she was scared. And her anger was like a volcano on the verge of erupting.

It didn't take long for Daniel to arrive, and Lanier greeted him with a cup of coffee.

"Thanks," he said, accepting the hot liquid.

They sat down on the sofa. The silence grew tight with tension. "I think he used a voice changer app or device," she stated after a moment. There was something off about the way the caller had sounded.

"I spoke with the employee working the front desk," Daniel said. "He said the caller just asked for you by name and to be connected to your room. The clerk said they do not give out room numbers."

A cold knot formed in her stomach. "It was the unsub. *I know it.*"

"But why is he threatening you?"

"For some reason he doesn't want me on this case. Something about my presence scares him." It might explain why the unsub hadn't gone after the other investigating officers.

Daniel looked perplexed. "It just doesn't make sense. He seems to be targeting you specifically, and we need to find out why."

Lanier didn't respond. Her mind was racing. *Does the unsub know what Daniel doesn't know? That Gayle Giraud is my mother? If so, is he going to try to use this information as some type of leverage?*

Her nerves tensed immediately.

"Lanier, are you okay?"

The tight knot within her begged for release. "Daniel, do you mind staying here? The sofa pulls out into a bed. I…"

"Absolutely. I'd feel more comfortable knowing that you're safe," he responded.

"Thank you." Lanier paused a heartbeat, then said, "I'm more angry than scared."

"I understand," he responded. "Getting a phone call like that would unnerve me."

She fought back tears. "I'm not going to allow this murderer to victimize me."

"You're no one's victim," Daniel assured her. "You're one of the two strongest people I know. My mom is the other person."

Lanier took a deep breath and tried to relax. "Thank you. That's quite a compliment."

"Why don't you go back to bed?" Daniel urged. "Get some sleep."

She gave a slight nod.

"Tomorrow, we're going to get a device to record any calls coming into this room," he said.

Lanier left him in the living room and climbed into bed. But she tossed and turned most of the night, restless.

At some point, she would have to tell Daniel what she'd been hiding. She hated keeping him out of the loop. Lanier hoped that when she did come clean, he would understand why it was so important for her to work this investigation.

Lanier deliberately put her need to solve the murders ahead of her growing feelings for Daniel. She refused to allow herself to be distracted—even though the thought of him outside her door last night, watching over her, made that difficult. It was nice having someone to protect her for a change.

She typed Robert Durousseau's name into the Google search bar, pulling up every article she could find on the man. Like his son, Robert's philanthropic endeavors were numerous, his efforts lauded by many worldwide.

She discovered that despite his family's wealth, Robert spent most of his teens in a reformatory school for car theft and manslaughter, but nonetheless had become the successful owner of a chain of high-end furniture stores and gained a reputation as a first-class upholsterer, taking over his father's upholstery business upon his death.

Why am I doing this? I should be focusing on the Crescent City Strangler.

Reluctantly, Lanier returned her attention back to the cold case files. She'd gone through hundreds of pages of notes, reading through the cases in chronological order to determine how the killer's MO might have grown and changed compared to the MO for the most recent murders. She was reviewing the murder book of Anna Jacobs, a stripper. Anna had been murdered a few weeks before her mother.

Nothing special stood out until she read through the crime scene notes. A set of fingerprints from the site where the body was found belonged to a man named Jesse Miller.

What captured her attention was that the suspect worked for Robert Durousseau. Jesse was considered a potential suspect but was never officially charged with Anna's murder. In fact, he was cleared because he had a solid alibi for the night the woman disappeared.

Lanier released a sigh of satisfaction. Her instincts hadn't failed her.

Her gut told her there was a link between Robert's disappearance and the victims. But in what way were they connected?

Lanier picked up the photograph of Jesse, staring at his face. He seemed familiar to her. Then it dawned on her. She remembered seeing him at one of the bars the night of her accident. The one where her mother used to work.

He could've easily followed her from the bar and crashed into her. He may have been the one who was watching her in the shadows.

Are you the serial killer we've been looking for all this time?

She watched the twenty-year-old video of the investigators interrogating him after Anna died. He told them that he'd been working for Robert the night of Anna's murder.

Her case files indicated that Robert confirmed it as the truth.

Lanier stole a peek out the one window in her office. Dark clouds were gathering overhead, threatening rain. The weather couldn't dampen her mood, though. She'd found a grain on the trail, and she believed it would lead her to the identity of the Crescent City Strangler.

She beckoned Daniel back to her office. "Close the door behind you, please."

He did as Lanier requested. "What's going on?"

"Do you recognize him?" she asked, holding up the photograph of Jesse Miller. "He's older now but looks the same."

"We saw him at one of the bars, right?"

"Yes. He was at the one where Gayle Giraud worked. Oh, and one more thing…this man worked for the Durousseau family as a driver and mechanic. He lived in an apartment over the garage on their estate."

Daniel's brows rose in surprise. "So Michael must know him?"

She nodded. "His fingerprints were on some evidence found in the Anna Jacobs investigation." That discovery had shocked her, too. Why would Michael not tell them? Or had a younger Michael not known? Lanier looked at Daniel. "I know this isn't what you want, but we are going to have to speak to Michael about this."

He agreed.

Thunder rumbled in the distance, and massive raindrops began to fall. She glanced outside. People on the street started walking briskly while others opened umbrellas to protect themselves from the downpour.

"I've never liked the rain." Lanier wrapped her arms around herself. "Some people find it comforting and relaxing, but I don't. It makes me anxious." The day the police notified her grandmother of Gayle's death, it had been rainy, dreary and dark. Almost ominous. Days like this, when the weather was gray, reminded her of that tragic moment in time.

"Why is that?" Daniel asked.

Lanier wasn't sure how to respond.

Daniel assessed her. "I spoke with my mother, and I was thinking you should stay with her."

"Daniel, no…" Lanier protested. "I can't do that. It was just a phone call. If he calls again, it'll be recorded. I'm not running away. I feel like we must be getting close."

"Someone crashed into you, and now you've received a threat by phone—we don't know why he's after you, but I'm gonna find out."

Daniel and Lanier stood in the doorway of Lanier's office. "Michael…" He was not at all looking forward to this conversation. Hopefully it would not come off as an interrogation. He didn't want there to be tension between him and his partner. It unsettled him that Michael had never mentioned that a suspect in their investigation used to work for his family—but if Michael was shielding difficult memories of his past, Daniel could understand.

Michael joined them in the office where they all sat down.

"What's up?" he asked. "Y'all got something?"

"We're not really sure," Lanier said. "We're hoping you can help."

"Sure," Michael responded. "I'll do what I can."

Lanier held up the photo of Jesse. "You know this man?"

Michael's expression remained neutral. "Yeah, I do. He used to work for my father. His name is Jesse Miller." Michael paused, looking from Lanier to Daniel. "I'm confused. What does he have to do with the cases you're working on?"

"Did you ever meet Anna Jacobs?"

Michael looked genuinely confused. *"Who?"*

"Anna Jacobs," Lanier repeated.

"No," Michael responded. "She's one of the cold case victims, right? How would I have ever met her?"

"When Anna's body was found, Jesse was questioned and let go. Your father was his alibi."

Michael shrugged nonchalantly. "He lived in the apartment above the garage on the estate back then. My father worked him long hours. Jesse maintained our cars, drove us wherever we had to go, and did whatever else my father needed him to do. He was basically a live-in handyman."

"Are you in contact with your father or Jesse?" Lanier asked.

"I get an email from time to time from Robert." So he did keep up with his dad. "I haven't talked to Jesse in a while. Even then, it was only in passing. I remember he loved to drink."

"Why did your father leave town?" she asked.

Michael looked her straight in the eye. "Robert embezzled millions from his own company and abandoned his only child. I consider it a blessing that we were able to keep this out of the news and I was able to sell the business for a nice profit after what he did."

An embezzlement scandal? That would certainly explain why he'd skipped town so fast. "I don't wish to bring up painful memories," Lanier stated.

"Right now, our focus should be Jesse Miller," Daniel interjected. "We need to talk to him about Anna Jacobs and see what comes of it."

Lanier agreed.

"He's a mechanic," Michael offered. "I heard he's working at some shop in Algiers Point."

Lanier turned, grabbed her tote and headed to the door. "Let's find Miller and have a conversation."

Daniel and Lanier located Jesse at his workplace. They decided it was best that Michael not be involved at this point. Lanier was concerned about just how open

Jesse would be with the son of his former employer present.

Noting the man's sallow skin and bloodshot, dull eyes, she suspected he was either a functional alcoholic or drug addict.

"What do you want with me?" he asked, glancing from Lanier to Daniel but not looking directly at them. "I ain't done nothing wrong."

"We'd like to talk to you about Anna Jacobs," Lanier stated.

Jesse popped a mint into his mouth. "What about her?"

The peppermint did nothing to mask the suspicious odor on his breath, forcing her to take a step backward. "We're reopening her case. We know you were on the suspect list at one point."

"The police cleared me." Jesse wiped his hands on an oil-stained towel.

"We're aware of that," Daniel responded. "A lot of years have passed. We were hoping that maybe now you remember something more that can help us. It was noted in Anna's case files that she was romantically involved with you. Is this correct?"

Jesse's shoulders slumped. "I loved her."

"Do you know if she was afraid for her life?" Lanier asked.

"She wasn't," Jesse answered. "Anna would've told me."

Lanier switched her tote from one shoulder to the other. "I'm curious. How did you meet Anna?"

"I worked for the richest man in New Orleans. Everybody thought he was this great man, but the truth is that Robert Durousseau was arrogant, controlling and cold-hearted. He would bring women—strippers and prostitutes—to the guesthouse." Jesse shrugged. "I think it excited him to have sex with other women while his wife was sleeping in the main house. Anna was a working girl back then. She was one of his favorites. When Robert finished with 'em, I'd give 'em money and take 'em home."

Jesse wiped his hands once more on the soiled cloth. "Anna and I used to talk during the drive. We had a lot in common. One thing led to another, and we fell in love. Anna loved me so much that she gave up that life so we could be together."

"Did she have a pimp?" Daniel inquired.

Jesse shook his head. "She worked for herself. Anna was smart." He paused a moment, then said, "Robert was furious when she told him she was out of the business. One day he walked in on us in my bed. He fired me. Anna turned up missing two days later. They didn't find her body for four days." Tears welled up in his eyes.

"Do you believe Robert had something to do with her disappearance?" Lanier questioned.

"He was ruthless and thought he was smarter and better than everyone else," Jesse uttered. "I confronted Robert the day Anna disappeared and asked him straight out. I reminded him how I used to protect him when we were in reformatory school together. He told me to leave his property, or he'd have me thrown in jail."

Daniel opened his mouth to speak, but Lanier gave a slight shake of her head. She then asked, "Do you know anything about his disappearance?"

"No, I don't." Jesse glanced over his shoulder, then back at them. "I better get back to work. Anna's been gone a long time. I really hope you find the killer."

"Did you happen to know Gayle Giraud?"

He shrugged. "I meet a lot of people as a mechanic. I'm better with faces."

"She was killed not too long after Anna."

"That's right…there was another girl… I was heart-broken over Anna back then."

Her stomach sank. She wished he'd remembered something about her mother. "If you can think of anything else, please don't hesitate to reach out to us."

He nodded. "I gotta get back to work."

When they were seated in the car a few moments later, Daniel said, "According to his statement, Jesse told the police that he was working the night Anna went missing. Robert said the same thing, but he just told us he was already fired by then."

"*Exactly.* He lied, and so did Robert," Lanier responded. "Why would you give an alibi for someone you fired?"

"That's what we need to find out."

She glanced over at him. "At first, I thought he was twitchy because of abusing alcohol or drugs, but he almost seemed afraid. I'm beginning to think Jesse's hiding something. We just have to keep pressing him—we know he's not a good liar."

"Right now, Jesse is our strongest lead. They were both involved with Anna Jacobs. We just found out that Jesse's alibi for that night was a lie," Daniel summarized. "As for Robert, he was never a suspect, but we have no idea where he was the night Anna was murdered."

Chapter Sixteen

$\sim$

It was past five o'clock. Daniel and Lanier sat in one of the conference rooms discussing the current cases. He leaned forward in his chair as she put up the timeline of the women's disappearances and the discoveries of the bodies on a whiteboard.

He listened intently, and every so often, Daniel felt an almost electric feeling when her gaze landed on him. He'd never felt such an emotional connection with anyone.

"The canal is the dumping ground," he stated. "The earlier victims were placed all along the canal, but not in the same general area as the four found recently."

Lanier sat down at the table across from him. "I wish there was a way to track both Robert's and Jesse's whereabouts on the days these women went missing. What about the other four victims? We need to know what Jesse was doing on the nights they disappeared."

"We need to have another conversation with him, then," Daniel said.

"I didn't say anything earlier because I'm just not buying that Jesse Miller killed all these women," she responded. "I *do* believe he knows something—he may even know the identity of the unsub. He strikes me as the type who barks but doesn't really bite. However, I could be wrong about him."

"We can put a tail on him."

"Not yet," Lanier said. "We should check to see if he has an alibi for the nights all four women were killed. Let's just start there."

"I'll stop by the shop tomorrow morning."

"Why wait?" Lanier asked. "Let's go back now. He may be still there." She stood up. "I'll ride with you and leave the rental here. I can Uber to the station in the morning."

"I don't mind picking you up tomorrow," he said.

They drove to Algiers Point together. Jesse was preparing to leave when they pulled up. Daniel blocked his vehicle by parking behind it.

He looked surprised to see them again, then irritated. "What do y'all *want* now?"

Daniel stepped out of the car. "Jesse, we have a couple more questions."

"I told y'all everything I know. What happened to Anna was a long time ago."

"Do you know any of the four women that were found recently?" Lanier asked.

"No. Why are you asking me about them? Because I was involved with Anna? Now you think I'm the one who's killing these women."

Lanier shrugged. "We have to cover our bases."

"Can you tell us where you were on the dates in question?" Daniel inquired.

"Every evening I work on cars for people who can't afford to pay what I have to charge at the shop. It's my side hustle. I keep a calendar," Jesse said. "It has names, what I charged and what time I worked. It's in my car if you'd like to see it."

They walked with him to the black Camry, and Jesse presented the calendar.

"Do you mind if I take a picture of this?" Lanier asked.

"Do what you gotta do."

She took photographs of several months, then said, "Thank you for your help. This should resolve any questions we have. Enjoy your evening."

When they were in the car, Lanier looked at the photographs. "Looks like he stays busy. We just need to verify that he was really working on cars the nights the women were murdered."

Daniel hoped they were not heading down a road that would lead to a dead end. He could tell that Lanier wasn't convinced Jesse was their killer, but they couldn't exactly rule him out.

They had to examine every angle.

When Daniel arrived at her suite later, he found Lanier had exchanged her navy pantsuit for a pair of jeans and a casual T-shirt. Her long curly hair flowed free. He liked her relaxed look, a contrast to her usual hyper-focused attitude. Seeing her like this ignited emotions Daniel hadn't experienced in years. Yet he forced the idea of them being anything other than coworkers out of his mind. It was hard for Daniel to sit by and watch someone he loved placing themselves in dangerous situations. His first thought was always to protect the people he cared about.

He glanced over at Lanier. Daniel believed her very

capable of taking care of herself, but it would be a struggle to sit back without coming to her aid if she was ever in danger. He would put himself in the line of fire to keep her safe. *Just like before.* Daniel was able to keep his focus by avoiding romantic entanglements in the workplace.

"I ordered a pizza. I hope that's okay," she said.

"Works for me," he responded. They'd agreed to work through dinner. After speaking with Jesse earlier, he knew they were getting closer to finding their murderer. He knew Lanier felt it too. While they waited for the food, she set up an easel and paper.

"Let's start from the beginning and work forward," Lanier suggested. "With the first known victim of the Crescent City Strangler." She posted a photo of the woman on the paper and jotted down her name. "This is Monique Vega. She was a thirty-four-year-old prostitute. She lived in Tremé. We know that she got into a car and was missing for ten days. The only thing we know about the car is that it was black. No one could give a definitive description back then of the type."

"And no one paid attention to the license plate?" Daniel asked.

"It's not noted anywhere. One of the witnesses said there were so many black cars picking up girls every night. No one paid attention."

"She didn't have a pimp?" Daniel asked. "No protection?"

"All of the victims seemed to work without pimps, or they worked in strip clubs."

Lanier posted a photo of the second victim. They discussed the similarities to the first before moving on to the third.

When the pizza arrived, they sat down to eat.

She wiped her mouth on a paper napkin before saying, "You'll see that the MO changes when we get to victim thirteen. That's when the unsub began using rope."

"I guess it was becoming harder for him to strangle the women by hand," Daniel said before biting into his slice of pepperoni pizza.

"I'm not sure why he switched," Lanier responded. "But he decided to use garrotes with a knot in the middle to crush their larynx. These victims also had bruising on their backs which suggests that the unsub used a knee or foot."

"Maybe he was worried about leaving behind DNA that could identify him."

She considered his words. "You may have a point. Because it seems he also started using gloves around that time."

Daniel got up and grabbed two bottles of water from the mini-fridge. She moved back to the couch and made herself comfortable.

He watched her every move, swallowing how her nearness affected him. He found himself powerless to resist the emotions she evoked within him. Daniel wanted to protect Lanier, to love her. Still, he tried valiantly to fight against his growing feelings for her. It was a challenge, working so closely together.

"Where did you grow up?" Daniel inquired, hoping to strike up a conversation that had nothing to do with work.

"In Richmond," Lanier responded. "I was adopted by my aunt and uncle after my parents died."

"I lost my father when I was ten."

Her brow furrowed, and she nodded. "I miss my parents so much," she said, almost to herself.

Daniel set his drink on the table. "I know exactly how you feel. It's been hard on my mom. She still bakes a cake each year for his birthday."

Lanier smiled. "I always buy a chocolate cupcake on my mom's birthday. It was her favorite."

They spent the next hour continuing to go through the cold cases. Lanier posted the photo of Gayle Giraud last. "She was twenty-four years old. She wasn't a prostitute or a stripper. Gayle worked as a bartender in the evenings so she could attend nursing school during the day."

"She and two of the other cold case victims had children, right?" he asked.

"Yes."

Lanier got up and tacked up photos of the four recent victims. She then added a photo of Abra, the woman who'd escaped her assailant.

"The question on the table is, why these women?" Daniel asked, indicating the photos of the most recent victims. "They don't appear to have anything in common with the others."

"They are all between the ages of twenty-four and thirty-five. The unsub removed their wedding rings..."

"Souvenirs." Lanier ran her fingers through her hair. "What are we missing?" she asked in frustration.

"They all have husbands," Daniel offered, "but one was in the middle of a divorce, and another was separated."

"Abra was having an affair," Lanier stated. "Ebony mentioned that with her husband away so much, Abra would get lonely, so she started talking to men online.

She says that Marcus is the only guy her friend actually met in person."

"Do you believe her?" he asked.

"I don't think Abra told Ebony everything," Lanier responded. "But I can't be sure."

Arms folded, she stared at the photos of the women. Daniel could sense her irritation in wanting to bring closure to this investigation. He felt it, too. But he was grateful that there hadn't been any more missing women.

He felt Lanier's gaze shift to him. Alone with her in this suite, Daniel had to fight his overwhelming need to find a reason—any reason—just to sit and talk with Lanier about anything other than work, but he drank in the comfort of her nearness. What he felt for her was different—it defied definition.

Lanier was very aware of Daniel's attraction to her. The emotional tension was thick and threatened to overtake the room. She fought against its talon-like grip by focusing on the women whose photographs were attached to the whiteboard. She refused to allow herself to lose control over her feelings. Lanier had learned at a young age that it was better to not love anyone than to love and have another person taken from her.

"Only one of the women didn't have on a wedding ring…" Daniel was saying.

"The one getting the divorce?" she asked.

He gave a slight nod.

Their eyes met and held, making Lanier nervous.

She detected a flicker in his intense eyes, causing her pulse to skitter alarmingly. Lanier couldn't recall ever wanting to kiss a man as much as she wanted to kiss Daniel. The anticipation was almost unbearable.

He stared with longing at her.

Lanier cleared her throat noisily, ignoring Daniel's tender appeal. "Maybe we should call it a night. It's almost one o' clock in the morning."

"I hadn't realized it was so late," he responded, almost apologetically.

She walked him to the door. "I'll see you later at the station."

His steady gaze bore into her. "Good night—or should I say good morning?"

Lanier grinned. "Both. Be safe, Daniel."

He left her feeling conflicted in her emotions. Lanier didn't have much dating experience, but she couldn't even think about anything else other than justice for her mother and the other women.

She sat staring at the whiteboard with the photographs of the victims.

Why my mother? She wasn't a prostitute or stripper. She worked near the area considered the red-light district, but in one of the bars. *Why was she targeted?*

She picked up a folder containing a dossier on Robert Durousseau and opened it.

Robert's birth mother was a prostitute who had abandoned him when he was a baby. He was adopted by the Durousseau family when he was a year old. However, the elder Durousseau later confessed he was Robert's biological father. The abandonment of his mother and the deception of his father could have triggered him in some way to start killing women who reminded him of his biological mother—a woman he hated.

He figured into this puzzle somehow—she just hadn't quite comprehended his part in it. Yet. Lanier wasn't giving up until she had all the pieces in place.

Chapter Seventeen

Lanier had just walked into her office when Michael walked out of the break room, coffee in hand.

"Good morning," he greeted in passing.

"Hey Michael." Lanier dropped her tote in her desk chair, then walked over to his desk. "I've been thinking about your father. It would be nice if we could talk to him about Jesse. Do you think you could reach out?"

"I could try," Michael responded. "I hear from him every now and then. The truth is that I'm not interested in having a relationship with him."

Lanier eyed him in surprise.

Michael shrugged. "We've never been close. He's always been an absentee father. He traveled a lot for buying trips or vendor and sales meetings. Whenever Robert did come home, I couldn't wait for him to leave again. Since he's been gone, life has been great for me." Michael glanced over his shoulder to see if anyone was paying attention to them.

"Do you have any idea where he could be?"

"Lanier, I don't care to know," Michael said, eyeing her. "I want him to stay out of my life."

She didn't know what to say, so she kept quiet.

"Robert left a long time ago. I prefer to just leave well enough alone."

"One day I'm going to learn to mind my own business," Lanier muttered under her breath as she walked back to her office. It was obvious that Michael's relationship with his father was strained and a sore subject for him.

Lanier liked him a lot and didn't want there to be any tension between them, so she hoped she wouldn't have to mention Robert's name ever again to Michael.

Deciding to take a midmorning break, Lanier picked up the apple on her desk and bit into it.

"Hey, there you are," a woman stated, strolling into her office. "FedEx just dropped this off for you."

"I didn't think you were working today, Tracy," she said.

"I have a son in college. I need all the overtime I can get."

They chatted for a few minutes before the front desk supervisor left and she opened the package, peeked inside and smiled. It was a gift from Celine. Her friend often sent little gifts to cheer her up—and Celine likely thought she needed it after visiting her mother's grave.

Lanier tossed the half-eaten fruit into the trash, grabbed the wallet out of her tote and strolled out of her office. She stepped outside of the station and walked across the street to a corner café because she craved beignets and chai tea.

She placed her order, then settled down at a bistro table inside since it was too chilly to sit outside. Lanier felt a few minutes away from the station would do her some good. Her heart broke repeatedly with each victim as she read their files.

Where was God when these poor women needed His protection? This question hammered at her.

"I guess you and I had the same idea," Daniel said from behind her.

"Seems so," Lanier responded. His nearness made her senses spin. She needed to put some distance between them. It was a good thing her order was called up and she went to grab it. "See you back at the station," she said to Daniel when she passed him.

Just as she stepped off the curb, a dark vehicle came barreling toward her. Frozen with fear, Lanier tried to urge her body to move but failed. Someone grabbed her, pulling her out of harm's way.

She glanced around. A crowd of people had gathered, asking if she was all right. It was Daniel who'd saved her. "Are you okay?" he asked, helping her sit up on the sidewalk. He'd managed to save her beignets along with her—but the tea had fallen in the scuffle.

Michael pushed through the sea of people. "What happened here?"

The shock that someone had driven a car straight at her hit Lanier full force. "Someone just tried to run me over," she responded shakily. Unsettled, Lanier tried to gather her memories, but everything had happened so fast.

"I'll take you to the hospital," Daniel said. "You need to get checked out."

She snatched her arm away from his grip. "I don't want to go anywhere," Lanier insisted. "I'm fine."

"Your arm's bleeding."

"They're just minor cuts. I may need a Band-Aid or two." She eyed him. "If I were a man, would you be so attentive? I don't think so. I keep telling you that I'm not some fragile being. I've had worse taking down a suspect," Lanier responded irritably.

She knew she was being unfair, but she was furious they didn't have anything to go on—it happened so fast that she didn't see the type of vehicle or the driver. All she knew was the color was a bright blue with tinted windows.

She eyed Daniel. "Did you notice anything about the car?"

"Just that it was missing a license plate," he responded.

"Jesse Miller has access to all types of cars," Daniel stated. "He repairs body work."

"You're thinking that he could've been the one who crashed into me?"

He nodded. "It's a possibility so it's worth a second look at him."

She nodded. She was sure he could see the discomfort written on her face after the accident but she appreciated that Daniel didn't try to push back on her refusal to go to the hospital. Though her entire body ached, Lanier knew she was going to have to put her pain aside. She counted on pure adrenaline to get her through the rest of the day.

At least she hoped it would.

"We need to go see Jesse Miller," Daniel told Michael when he escorted Lanier back inside the station.

His partner grabbed his coat. "Right behind you."

While Michael drove, Daniel thought over Lanier's words about being so protective when it came to her.

Lanier could take care of herself. He had to consider that he treated female officers differently than he would a man. This new awareness would now force him to make some changes in his actions.

"How are we going in?"

Michael's words drew Daniel away from his thoughts.

"First, we need to find out if he left his job at any point today and at what time. So I think we should speak to his employer first."

"Works for me."

"Do you believe Miller is capable of running down an FBI agent and killing women?" Daniel asked.

Shrugging, Michael responded, "To be honest, I don't know what to think right now. I'm still trying to process everything…like Robert and Jesse being involved with the same woman. I'm not sure I believe it. My father was a snob. He'd never stoop so low as to mess with the same person as his driver. I'm no fan of Robert, but it sounds to me like Jesse's trying to intentionally shift blame to my father."

"Lanier and I both got the feeling that Jesse was hiding something the day we talked to him."

Michael parked the vehicle in one of the empty parking spaces at the shop. They walked past the four vehicle bays where several mechanics were busy working on cars. The smell of oil hung in the air, assaulting their nostrils.

Daniel looked around but didn't see Jesse. "Doesn't look like he's here."

The manager approached them in a stained, faded gray jumpsuit. "What can I do to help you?" he asked.

"We're looking for Jesse Miller," Michael stated.

"He's at lunch. Won't be back for about half an hour."

"When did he leave?"

Scratching his head, the manager answered, "No more than ten or fifteen minutes ago."

"Are you sure about this?" Daniel asked.

"Yeah. I talked to him right before he left."

"If what he told us is true, the driver couldn't have been Jesse," Michael said when they were back in the car.

Daniel glanced around. "There isn't a car here that looked like the one that almost hit Lanier."

Michael pointed toward the parking lot two blocks away. "Does that look like it might be the car?"

"Drive over there. I need to see if it has a license plate."

Daniel sighed in frustration when he saw the tag on the back. "Run the tags. I want to know everything about that car. We may need to talk to the owner as well."

He and Michael got out and walked into the bakery.

"Who owns the blue Kia outside?" Daniel asked.

"I do," said a young girl behind the counter.

"What's your name?"

"Sherry Jackson. What's going on?"

"Has your car been parked in that same spot all day?" Michael inquired.

"Yessir," she answered.

Daniel walked up to the counter and showed his badge. "Are you sure it wasn't moved at all?"

"I had my brakes fixed this morning at the shop across the street. One of the mechanics dropped it off there, and it's been in that spot since."

"Was Jesse Miller the mechanic who worked on your car?" Michael wanted to know.

"Yessir. That was him. He always works on it for me.

He just did some body work on the car a month ago when some drunk rear-ended me."

"Thank you," Daniel said.

"Sir, why you askin' about my car?" Sherry asked.

Daniel didn't know her relationship with Jesse, so for now he didn't want to give her a chance to warn the mechanic. "A car that color was involved in an accident."

"It wasn't me. I've been here at work all day."

He smiled. "You have a great day."

"We got him," he stated when they got back into the car. "Let's just wait here for Jesse to return from lunch."

"What all do you know about Jesse Miller?" Daniel asked while they waited.

"I remember my father saying that he was always in trouble as a teen," Michael said. "In fact, Robert and Jesse met when he was in reformatory school."

"They have a long history together, then."

"A turbulent one," Michael said. "They weren't friends—they just tolerated one another. Robert gave him a job that paid well, so I guess that's why Jesse stayed as long as he did."

"If they didn't get along, why would your father hire someone he clearly despised? That doesn't make sense to me."

"Robert once told me that some of the other boys would try to jump him, and Jesse defended him. A lot of the boys at the reformatory school were afraid of Jesse. I guess Robert felt he owed him, so he gave him a job."

Michael glanced at Daniel. "I don't think he's coming back to work. He should've been back by now. He's on the run."

"Now we have to deliver this news to Lanier. She is not gonna be happy about this at all."

* * *

While they were gone, Lanier received an email from a forensic accountant with the bureau confirming that five million dollars had been transferred from the Durousseau business into an account overseas and withdrawn a few days later. That would explain his sudden disappearance after her mother died. It was because of an embezzlement scandal—nothing that proved he'd been involved with the murders.

What is going on here? she wondered. *How does Robert fit into all this*?

Michael had already been through so much, and now a former employee of his father could be the killer they'd been looking for all this time.

It was days like this that Lanier didn't enjoy being in law enforcement—when it affected a good person like Michael. She knew Daniel would be a strong support system for his partner.

She desperately wanted them to find the person who had tried to run her over.

Lanier was more than ready for this investigation to conclude, so that she could try to have some sort of a normal life. As much as she wanted to believe Jesse was behind the murders, she still felt there was a huge missing piece of the puzzle.

When Daniel and Michael returned, she rushed to her feet and went to meet them. "What happened?"

"According to his boss, he was at the shop at the time," Daniel responded. "We waited for him to return from lunch, but he didn't. We found the car—it belonged to a young girl working across the street. She told us she'd dropped it off this morning to have the brakes repaired. Jesse parked it in the spot where we found it."

"Did it have a license plate on it?" Lanier asked.

"Yeah."

"We went by Jesse's house, and he wasn't there," Michael stated. "He's from West Baton Rouge Parish. He may head there."

"We put a BOLO on him," Daniel said.

"So you still think he was the person driving the car that tried to hit me?"

"I do. I'm having CSI dust the blue car for prints."

Lanier turned on the large monitor on the wall in her office, which displayed a document. "This is Jesse's criminal record. When he was ten, he got in trouble for choking another kid on the playground. He was caught shoplifting on his thirteenth birthday. At fifteen, he set fire to the house of his ex-girlfriend, whose parents forbade her to see him. The girl was thirteen at the time, and her parents wouldn't allow her to see him outside of school. That's when he was sent to reformatory school."

Daniel noted that Jesse had gotten into several fights while there. "When we went back to talk to his boss, the man admitted he didn't really know when Jesse left—only that he said he was dropping off the customer's vehicle and then going straight to lunch."

"My gut tells me Jesse's not returning to the shop today," Lanier said. "He's planning his next move."

Along with Baton Rouge police officers, Daniel, Michael and Lanier entered the house where Jesse had grown up in bulletproof vests, guns drawn.

"Clear!" she shouted after she'd scanned her surroundings.

Daniel echoed the same as he moved through the

small house. A flash of irritation ripped through Lanier when they found it empty. Jesse wasn't there. No one had lived in the home for years, but they did find evidence proving that someone had been there recently.

"He's probably been staying here," Lanier said.

Daniel glanced around the house. "He's most likely long gone now."

Michael headed to the door. "I'll go talk to the neighbors next door and across the street."

Lanier pointed to a discarded shirt, a small pizza box and a cup. "We need to have all that stuff DNA tested."

One of the officers gently picked up the items with a gloved hand and placed them in plastic evidence bags. He sealed them in their presence.

Michael returned. "Jesse was definitely here. The neighbor across the street identified him. Said he's known him since he was a kid. The lady next door hasn't lived there long, but said she saw a man here. Her description matched Jesse. Tall, muscular, with locs down to his waist. She said she saw him leave about an hour ago."

"Do you think he's going to return?" Lanier asked.

"No idea, but his neighbors agreed to call if he does," Michael responded.

"If he happened to see all the police cars outside, he's definitely on the run now," she stated. "Do we even know what type of car he's driving?"

"A black Camry," Michael said. "It's registered to him."

"That could change," Daniel interjected.

The local police officers agreed to contact them if there were any sightings of Jesse Miller in the area.

Disappointed and frustrated, Lanier, Daniel and Michael made the hour and a half drive back to New Orleans.

Chapter Eighteen

Sarah came by the hotel to check on Lanier after hearing about the near hit-and-run.

"I'm fine," Lanier told her.

"You had to be terrified after something like that."

"It scared me for a moment," Lanier confessed. "Then I got angry."

"Do you think you were targeted?" Sarah inquired.

Lanier decided to keep her suspicions within the police station. "It was probably someone who lost control of their car. I'm hungry. Why don't you join me for a meal in the hotel restaurant?"

"Sure."

They took the elevator downstairs. Lanier scanned the dining area, which was filled with locals and tourists. It was convenient for hotel guests, but it was also a favorite among the people of New Orleans. She could understand why. The soft lighting was warm and inviting. The breathtaking artwork hanging on the walls in vivid hues added to its charm. Fresh flowers were placed in vases on the tables every day to welcome patrons.

"I met someone," Sarah announced. "His name is

Curtis, and he's so handsome. I truly treats me like a queen. I joined a dating site—something I never thought I'd do. But after sifting through all the frogs, I found my prince."

"That's wonderful. I'm happy for you." Lanier picked up her menu, scanning it. "When did this happen?"

"We've been dating for a couple of weeks now. We see each other almost every day. When we don't, we talk."

"You just dived right into the pool, didn't you?"

Sarah grinned. "I did. Curtis and I have a great time together. He makes me laugh… Lanier, I really like him."

"I can see that. You're glowing."

"Really?"

Lanier nodded. "Have you told Daniel about him yet?"

"No, because I don't want him running a background check on Curtis. Daniel's very protective of the people he cares about."

"Yes, he is," she murmured. "But it's not a bad thing, Sarah. You really have to be careful these days."

"Maybe I'll give him a call when I get home."

A server walked over to take their orders.

When she left, Sarah eyed her and grinned. "Now tell me…how are things between the two of you?"

"Who? Me and Daniel?"

"Yes."

"He and I make a good team," Lanier stated. "There's nothing else going on between us. The best way to describe us is that we're forging a friendship."

Sarah shook her head. "I don't know what's wrong with the two of you. I can see that you care about each other."

"We're both focused on this case right now. I can't speak for Daniel, but I personally can't juggle a relationship and this investigation. Romance has to be on the back burner for now."

"Are you sure that's all it is?"

"There's more," Lanier admitted. "I have some issues I need to work on, but again… I need to focus all my energy on making sure we find out who's murdering women in your city."

"Well, even though you may not want to hear this—Lanier, you and Daniel belong together. I can feel it in my spirit."

She laughed. "Why don't we change the subject back to you and Curtis?"

Their food arrived.

Sarah chuckled. "Okay. I certainly don't mind telling you more about this wonderful man."

I'd rather talk about anything other than my relationship with Daniel. Lanier plastered on a smile while listening to her friend gush about her new boyfriend.

They continued to make small talk while they ate. Lanier enjoyed her meal and Sarah's company. So much that she ordered dessert and a cup of hot tea. When they finished, she and Sarah returned to her suite where they enjoyed more coffee and tea.

Sarah left shortly after 11:00 p.m.

Lanier walked her down and watched her drive away before taking the elevator back to her floor.

Lanier and Daniel were standing near his desk talking when they heard a woman speaking loudly.

"I need to speak to the person in charge of the murder investigation. If the Crescent City Strangler is back like people are saying, I might have some information. My sister was one of his victims."

"I guess we'd better hear what she has to say," Daniel said.

Lanier was already heading toward the reception desk.

Approaching the woman, she said, "Hi, I'm Special Agent Lanier Barrow, and this is Detective Daniel Jordan. And you are…"

"Charline King. Pansy Tremont was my sister. She was seeing that rich man—the one who went missing."

Lanier and Daniel exchanged a look of surprise before leading Charline to a conference room for privacy.

Once they were seated, Lanier asked, "Are you referring to Robert Durousseau?"

"Yeah. *Him.*"

Daniel leaned forward in his seat. "How do you know this?"

Charline pulled out a leather-bound book from her purse. "My sister kept journals. When she died, all of Pansy's stuff was put away in boxes and stored in my parents' attic. My mama died last month, and we've been cleaning out the house. I read some of her journals, and she talks about meeting that man. Robert. His driver used to pick her up and take her to their secret place— that's what she called it."

"First, we'd like to say sorry for your loss," Lanier said. "Our sincere condolences to you and your family."

"Thank you," Charline responded. "She had cancer, so we knew it was coming."

"Did Pansy ever mention the location of the secret place?" Daniel asked.

"Naw. She just said he paid her a lot of money for

sex, and he liked it rough. Pansy was an exotic dancer. I guess she did other stuff on the side."

"How many times did they meet up?" Lanier wanted to know.

"Looks like it was just three or four times before she was murdered. I don't know if it means anything, but I thought y'all should know. Both disappearing like that… it might be connected."

"Thank you for coming here, Charline. Do you mind if we keep the journal for evidence?"

"If it will help solve Pansy's murder, I don't care."

They walked Charline out before going to Lanier's office to talk.

"Robert had ties to Anna Jacobs and now Pansy Tremont." Lanier eyed Daniel. "I'm now wondering if he had ties to any of the other women."

"Jesse can answer that," he responded. "The women had no way of contacting Robert. But maybe Jesse knew something…"

"What about Michael? Maybe he saw something when he was younger."

Daniel shook his head. "I'm sure he would've said something if so. We should look to see if Robert kept an apartment or another piece of property somewhere in the city." He paused a moment, then said, "Are we really considering that Robert may be a piece of this puzzle?"

"We have no choice," Lanier responded.

"Hey, what's going on?" Michael said, entering the office. "Who was that lady that left a few minutes ago? I heard she talked to y'all."

"Her sister Pansy was a victim of the Crescent City Strangler. She recently came across a journal and brought it to us," Lanier said. She took a deep, cleansing breath, then continued. "Michael, there are entries in this journal about your father. Apparently, he slept with her several times before she was found murdered. Jesse seems to have transported her back and forth to some secret meeting place."

She surveyed the myriad emotions on Michael's face and assumed he was trying to process this new information about Robert. "I really hate to have to ask this, but were you ever aware of your father cheating on your mother? And do you know if he kept an apartment or another house locally?"

"Robert was gone a lot. My mother always suspected he had other women. I don't know anything about another place." Michael paused a moment. "Look, if he's involved in all this, you can count on me to do everything within my power to bring him to justice."

"Hey, I'm really sorry."

After a moment, Michael said, "I'm good. I just want answers like everybody else."

He left the office and went to speak briefly with their supervisor.

Michael returned a few minutes later and said, "I'll see y'all later. I'm going home. I need to be with my kids."

"He's not okay," Lanier said after she and Daniel watched him leave the building.

"Can you blame him?" Daniel responded. "He was just informed that his father may have something to do with yet another one of the victims—and maybe the murders."

"I want more than anything to be wrong about Robert, for Michael's sake, but my gut tells me otherwise."

* * *

"What's this?" Lanier asked when Michael handed her a small stack of letters the next day.

"The emails Robert sent to me," he responded.

She accepted them and began reading. They were all only a few sentences long, and each one was to the point—basically informing his son that he was doing well and traveling the world. Robert never once asked about his grandchildren. Michael had already told her that he didn't have a relationship with his father, so maybe his family was off-limits.

"Lanier, I need to know something…"

She looked up at Michael. "What is it?"

"Do you believe that Robert is behind the deaths of all these women? Is he the Crescent City Strangler?"

Lanier glanced at him. "The only thing we know right now is that he and Jesse are both connected to Pansy Tremont and Anna Jacobs. We suspect that Jesse is the one who tried to run me down—I suspect he's also the one who crashed into me. He's the only person that can provide more information, but he's suddenly disappeared."

"But do you think Robert and Jesse are working together?"

"I don't know, Michael. If we can locate Jesse, maybe we can find out what happened."

"I hope you find him," Michael said. "We all need answers."

Chapter Nineteen

On yet another night, Daniel joined Lanier in her suite to keep working on the case. They were close—but they were missing something. And they needed to figure it out. They ate Chinese takeout while they worked.

Daniel was finding it hard to keep his emotions at bay. He never considered that he'd fall for another woman in law enforcement. Despite keeping a professional distance, Daniel hadn't been prepared for the way Lanier made him feel.

Just being here in this room with her sent a course of electricity through him. Daniel tried to shake off the feeling of being so alive but was failing miserably.

After they finished their meal, Daniel and Lanier returned their focus to the stack of murder books on the coffee table.

"There's something we keep missing here," she stated in exasperation.

"Okay, so let's start with the one who got away," Daniel responded. "Abra worked at an IT company."

"She was married like all the other victims…"

"Married ladies who liked to party," Daniel contributed. "And they enjoyed flirting."

"Celine is a flirt," Lanier stated. "She always says that it's harmless. She's been in a committed relationship for four years. She never takes it any further than that… Abra was a flirt, but she was also having an affair." She eyed Daniel. "What about the other women? What if they took the flirting to another level? Abra met Marcus online. What if what they have in common is a profile on a dating site?"

"You're thinking they were cheating on their husbands?"

"I remember seeing an ad or something advertising a dating site for married people. I think it was called Discreet Affairs."

"I think we should check it out," Daniel said. "We should start by asking Abra the name of the site she used to meet Marcus. You talk to Abra, and I'll speak with Marcus."

"She's still out of town," Lanier responded. "I checked on her yesterday. She told me that she broke things off with Marcus. She and her husband are trying to work on their marriage."

"I'll reach out to Marcus first thing in the morning," Daniel said.

Their gazes caught, and Daniel couldn't look away. Feeling like there was a deeper significance to the interchange, he gently pulled Lanier toward him and kissed her.

She kissed him back. He wasn't sure of the exact moment when she changed from passive recipient to eager participant.

He kissed her a second time. Daniel's mouth covered hers tenderly until, reluctantly, he released her. "I'm sorry. I hope I haven't offended you," Daniel said quietly. "I have no idea what just came over me. I just know I wanted to kiss you."

"I wanted it, too," Lanier confessed.

Mixed feelings surged through him. He shouldn't have crossed that line—but he'd been wishing for that kiss for days.

Lanier cleared her throat. "Why don't we just pretend the kiss never happened. Our focus needs to be on the investigation."

He nodded stiffly, his senses reeling as if short-circuited, but he tried to display an outward calm. "Maybe we should call it a night."

Lanier readily agreed, and she escorted him to the door.

"I'm sorry for overstepping."

Lanier placed a hand to his mouth and said, "We're both adults. We're fine, Daniel. It just can't happen again."

"Agreed," he responded.

Yet Daniel felt a certain sadness at the thought that he'd never be able to kiss her again.

The next morning came much too quickly for Lanier, but it was time for her to get out of bed. She'd relived the kisses she shared with Daniel repeatedly in her mind for most of the night and was unable to sleep. Kissing him had been idyllic. But then reality hit her.

Nothing more can come of this—you can't afford to lose your heart to Daniel.

When the alarm went off a second time, Lanier

crawled from beneath the covers and made her way to the bathroom for a quick shower.

Emotions she didn't want to put a name to raged through her like a wildfire, but Lanier put on a charcoal-gray pantsuit beneath a gray plaid overcoat to ward off the cold weather. She fashioned her hair into a bun, then made her way down to the lobby.

Lanier left the hotel and drove to the station. She decided she'd follow Daniel's lead. If he acted as if nothing had happened between them, then so would she.

When she arrived, Daniel was already there. His morning greeting was strictly professional.

"I met up with Marcus, and he said he and Abra met on Discreet Affairs. They're based out of Baton Rouge, but we're not gonna get much information out of them without a subpoena, and then their lawyers are going to stall the process with a bunch of legal statutes. The company promises their clients complete anonymity."

"I can set up a profile on the site," Lanier suggested. "I can search to see if any of the recent victims had accounts with this particular company—if so, we've found our connection."

Daniel nodded in approval.

"Should I use my own photo?" Lanier asked as she set up the fake account.

"No." He got up and walked to the door. "Melba, can you come here for a moment?"

When she joined them in Lanier's office, Daniel gave her an overview of what they were looking for.

Melba worked sex crimes and already had several fictitious profiles set up, so she was immediately on board. "I'll send you one of my photos to upload. In the meantime, you may also want to check the victims' financials. I'm sure the company has a shell corporation under a more general name to bill their clients. Discreet Affairs would definitely be a red flag in a marriage."

"Thanks, Melba," Lanier said.

She set up an email and uploaded the photo to the profile. Once she was granted full access, Lanier was able to locate Marcus. "I can't find Abra's profile, but I'm betting she had an account with them at some point."

"Try Carolyn Mays," Daniel said.

"She's got one—it's still showing active." Lanier found profiles of the other three murdered women as well. "They're all here." She couldn't believe it—they'd finally found the missing link between the latest victims. On a whim, she decided to search one more person's name.

Jesse Miller.

She was stunned by what came up. "You're not going to believe this, Daniel."

He turned to her. "What?"

"Jesse has a profile on this site. I tried Robert's name just now, but nothing came up."

Daniel's brow furrowed. "This is no coincidence. We really need to find him."

"Who?" Michael asked when he entered the office.

"Jesse Miller," Daniel answered. "We just discovered all the victims and Jesse were members of an online dating site called Discreet Affairs."

Michael seemed as surprised as they were. "I just came to tell you that I sent Robert an email asking to see him. I'll let you know when I hear back."

"He's definitely someone we need to talk to," Daniel said. "He's known Jesse a long time. They have history." This was suddenly coming together so quickly... her mind raced, until she landed on one thought.

Daniel glanced at Lanier. "What's on your mind?" She knew he'd come to recognize that introspective look on her face.

"Maybe that's why the Crescent City Strangler stopped killing. He fell in love," Lanier stated. "Maybe he got married, but his wife cheated on him. Maybe she met someone online. Her infidelity triggered him to start killing again. That could be why the MO changed. This unsub exacted punishment on strippers and prostitutes in the past. This time it's women who were unfaithful."

"It's a great way to find targets," Daniel said with a smile. "You did it, Lanier. We have the trigger—he chooses local women who are unfaithful."

Daniel's reassuring smile, and the hand he placed on her shoulder, made her stomach flutter. He believed in her—and they were so close. But Lanier pushed all thoughts of him and their kiss to the back of her mind. She couldn't afford to be distracted, especially now that they were finally making headway with the investigation. They couldn't afford to let Jesse Miller slip away. He had to pay for his crimes.

"We've looked everywhere, and there's still no sign of Jesse," Daniel announced a few hours later. "His boss says he hasn't seen him since that day we came to the shop. He never returned from lunch. We have an APB out for him."

Lanier poured herself a cup of tea. "He'll turn up, and when he does—we'll find him."

A thick knot of emotions whipped through Daniel as he followed Lanier out of the break room—awe, respect and a distinct kind of pride he knew he had no right to feel.

He walked over to the whiteboard in the conference room, studying it. Daniel bit back his frustration. They'd had Jesse, and he'd let him go. "I never should've released him. This is on me."

"You're not to blame," Lanier said from the doorway. "We didn't have all the information at the time."

He placed his hands to his face. "I'm grateful there haven't been any more murders, at least."

"Jesse most likely left town because he knew we were closing in on him," she stated. "I'm wondering if Robert knew what was going on. Jesse tried to implicate his employer, but the man isn't here to defend himself."

"We really need to talk to Robert."

"Hopefully, Michael will get him to agree to chat with us."

Daniel gave a wry smile. "I hope it's soon. I don't want another woman ending up dead."

"I agree," Lanier responded.

"You need a life," Daniel blurted without thinking.

"Excuse me?"

"Outside of work, I mean. Since you've been in New Orleans, all I've seen you do is work."

"That's because we have a case to solve, Detective Jordan. Besides, you've pulled as many hours as I have on this investigation."

"That's why I'm speaking up now. I believe in a well-rounded lifestyle. We both need to walk away from all this for at least a few hours."

Lanier tried to assess his unreadable features. "So, what exactly are you suggesting?"

"That you and I call it a day and actually leave work when we're supposed to get off. Tomorrow, we'll be refreshed and able to think more clearly."

"I like it," she responded with a grin. "To be completely honest, I could use a break from all this, but we can't afford to lose time on this investigation."

Back at his desk, Daniel sat in disbelief. The thought had just come out of nowhere. Regardless, it had worked. He was tired, but a happy man.

It was true that they needed to regain clarity by putting some space between them and the investigation.

A tiny smile tugged at his lips. It wasn't at all a bad situation for either of them. It would also give him a chance to regain some emotional distance between himself and Lanier.

The next day, Lanier invited Daniel to work in her suite instead of the office. She didn't feel as comfortable discussing Robert Durousseau at the station, especially with Michael around.

Dressed in a dark pink turtleneck sweater and caramel-brown ponte knit pants tucked inside matching brown boots, Lanier opened the door shortly after eight a.m. to let Daniel enter her suite. She openly admired how handsome he looked.

Smiling, she said, "You look nice and relaxed."

He fingered a curling tendril of her hair. "So do you."

"I had a good night's sleep," Lanier said.

"Me, too."

"I really feel terrible for Michael," she said once they were seated on the sofa in the living room. "I wanted to work here to spare him the embarrassment."

"I figured as much," he responded.

They went back over the emails and everything they'd learned.

"He's not showing up anywhere," Lanier said. "Not in any country."

Daniel shook his head. "He must be using fake credentials."

She agreed.

They worked for six hours straight. Before he left, Daniel turned to her and asked, "Will you have dinner with me tonight?"

"Sure. What time?"

"Does seven work for you?"

Lanier smiled. "Sure. I'll see you then."

Neither of them said a word for the moment.

To break the silence, Lanier murmured, "I think I need to take a nap. We've had a very busy day."

As soon as Daniel left, she dropped down on the sofa and fell asleep for an hour. Then she showered, slipped on a robe, and sat down to curl her hair. Something was pressing on her mind. Daniel had not tried to kiss her at all. In fact, he seemed to be practicing great restraint in avoiding getting closer. Some of her hesitancy came from not wanting a distraction until they closed the pending cases. Also, she would eventually return home to Virginia, and she didn't believe in long-distance relationships.

When Lanier finished her hair, she got dressed, choosing an azure blue dress with silver studs around the neck and sleeves.

Daniel arrived promptly at seven, looking handsome in a black suit with a pearl-gray shirt and burgundy tie.

"Where are we going?" she asked when they were driving to their destination.

"Restaurant R'evolution."

"Is that the one at the Royal Sonesta New Orleans Hotel?"

He nodded. "Yeah. Have you been there already?"

"No, this will be my first time."

"Then you're in for a great dining experience," Daniel told her. "This is a favorite of mine."

They were seated promptly after their arrival.

He selected the blue crab beignets as an appetizer while they waited for their main entrées.

"Daniel, I'm going to be honest with you. I don't regret the kiss. I enjoyed it as much as you did. My only question is, why did you kiss me in the first place if it makes you so uncomfortable?"

"I couldn't help myself. I'm very attracted to you," Daniel confessed.

Lanier wiped her mouth on the end of her napkin. "Since we're being honest, I must admit that I'm attracted to you, too, but we need to keep our focus on the investigation."

"Do you think we can try to be friends, at least?"

She smiled. "Of course. I thought we already were."

"The thing is, I'm lying to you right now," Daniel stated. "I don't just want to be friends with you. I want more."

"I'm not right for you," Lanier said. "There are things you don't know about me."

"I've been telling myself this repeatedly, Lanier. It doesn't change how I feel about you."

"If I'm honest with myself, Daniel, I feel the same way, but we just can't go there. We can't set ourselves up for failure, and that's what we'd be doing."

Lanier took his hand in her own. "I value our friendship."

"As do I."

The server arrived with their meals. They ate mostly in silence, and afterward, Daniel took her back to the hotel.

"Thanks for today," Lanier told him. She planted a kiss on his cheek. "Drive safe."

"Good night," he murmured.

She walked through the lobby and took the elevator to her floor.

Lanier had been back in her room about fifteen minutes when a knock sounded on the door.

She stole a look through the peephole before unlocking it to let Daniel inside.

They stood staring at one another for a moment with longing. Then, without warning, he pulled her into his arms, kissing her. Daniel held her snugly.

A brief shiver rippled through Lanier, and she buried her face against the corded muscles of his chest. She had no desire to back out of his embrace.

He gazed down at her with tenderness. "This is much harder than I thought it would be."

Parting her lips, Lanier raised herself to meet his kiss. His lips pressed against hers, then gently covered her mouth, sending the pit of Lanier's stomach into a wild swirl. Daniel showered her with kisses around her lips and along her jaw.

This time, it was she who slowly pulled away. "I had a nice time with you, but I think we should say goodbye right now. *For real this time*."

"I agree."

"Good night, Daniel."

He turned to leave, then paused, asking, "Are you

going to the birthday party for Michael's daughter to-morrow?"

Lanier nodded. "He invited me."

"If you want, I'll come by and pick you up. It's on the way to his house."

"Sure," she responded. "I'd like that."

Staring at her reflection after he'd left, Lanier couldn't deny it any longer. She was falling in love with Daniel. And it scared her. When she thought of loving someone with her whole heart, the very idea of losing that person was something she didn't think she could survive.

This is no way to live.

Shaking off her insecurities, Lanier resolved to enjoy Sunday with Daniel with no expectations of anything more. She would enjoy these moments with him, and when it was time to leave, she would have no regrets.

Chapter Twenty

On the drive to Michael's house, Daniel said, "Jesse Miller is definitely on the run, but we'll find him."

"There's no way he could know that we're on to him, right?" Lanier asked.

"No, but a guilty man often takes precautions. They become paranoid, especially after a conversation with the police."

Lanier decided to change the subject. She held up a colorful gift bag. "I bought Michael's daughter a doll. I hope she likes it."

"She will," Daniel said. "Melinda loves them. I just went with a gift card to a toy store."

Lanier knew which house belonged to Michael because of the huge balloon display and all the cars parked in the driveway and in front of the house.

Daniel parked around the corner. "Looks like Melinda has a lot of friends."

"I never liked parties," Lanier said with a catch in her voice. "It wasn't the same without my parents there. We celebrated each year with a small cake and a family dinner. The one gift I wanted, I could never expect to receive, so it was basically just another day to me."

"Birthdays are huge in my family," Daniel responded. "Not quite on this scale, but they were nice."

They got out of the car and walked across the lawn, dodging children playing tag.

Michael was on the porch waiting for them. "I thought that was y'all. *Welcome to the party.*" He led them inside the historic home on Josephine Street in the Lower Garden District.

"Michael, you have a really beautiful home," Lanier murmured, looking around. She admired the lovely hardwood floors and windows that welcomed in tons of natural light. The second floor had a lot of balcony space and scenic French doors.

"Thank you. I wanted something a little smaller, but when Carly saw this house, she fell in love with it so I bought it."

She glimpsed a flicker of sadness in Michael's eyes. "Where should I put this gift?"

"We have a table over here."

Lanier sat down at a table with Daniel and some of the parents. She ate a burger and laughed as she watched Melinda and her friends playing games.

The scene made Lanier realize she hadn't had much of a childhood. Most of her youth had been spent reading books for entertainment when she wasn't studying. She couldn't blame her aunt or uncle—they'd tried to give her what they considered a normal life, but she rebelled. It wasn't until she met Celine in college that she started to loosen up.

Celine was the one who'd taken her to her first party and made sure no one offered her alcohol since she was underage. Having grown up with an alcoholic father, Celine never promoted drinking—she never touched it herself. Despite their eight-year age difference, they became the best of friends.

"You look like you're many miles away from here." Daniel's voice pulled Lanier out of her reverie. "Huh…"

"You seemed like you were deep in thought."

"I was thinking about my youth and how much I missed out on doing normal kid things."

"Any regrets?" he asked.

"Not really," Lanier responded. "I've enjoyed my life—it's not a bad one. I just wish I'd enjoyed my youth more."

One of the qualities that attracted Daniel to Lanier was her genuine smile, which always seemed prominently on display. She was nothing like the women he'd dated in the past. She didn't minimize her strength and didn't compromise her femininity. Still, there was a part of her Daniel believed she kept only to herself. Like she was doing right now. He wanted to know everything about her.

Daniel reminded himself that she was only going to be in New Orleans for a short time, so why not make the best of the time they had together?

After they'd left the party, Lanier invited Daniel up to her suite. They settled down on the sofa to watch television. She reached for the remote and turned down the volume.

Daniel eyed her. "What's up? You look like you have something on your mind?"

Lanier seemed mildly surprised that he could read her so well.

"I was thinking it might not be so bad for us to spend some time together as friends," she stated. "We always have a good time whenever we're together. Besides, I still need to teach you at least one line dance before I leave."

Her words were music to his ears.

"I'd really like that," Daniel said, his eyes never leaving her face. Stroking his chin, he added, "Believe it or not, I may not be able to dance, but I actually know how to have a good time."

"I know," she responded. "You've shown me a great time. That's why I enjoy your company. I feel safe with you, Daniel."

He leaned toward her, gazing into her eyes. "Do you really want to know what I enjoy doing?"

"I'm not sure I do…"

Daniel burst into laughter. "I enjoy reading mysteries. I also like going to art museums, exhibits, stuff like that. What do you enjoy doing?"

"I love the ocean, so I like spending a lot of time on a beach," Lanier responded. "I'm also a huge history buff—I'm always taking tours—and of course, I love music and dancing."

The warmth of his smile echoed in his voice. "Interesting… I love history myself," Daniel responded.

Her eyes shimmered with the light from the window. She gave him a smile that sent his pulse racing.

Daniel didn't want to think about the moment Lanier would have to return to Virginia. He didn't think he'd be able to just let her walk out of his life.

* * *

Two days later, Lanier and Daniel were just about to leave the station when a police officer stopped them by saying, "Jesse Miller's body was just found under a bridge."

Stunned by the news, she glanced over at Daniel and said, "I guess we'd better get over there." Apprehension swirled around her stomach as reality sank in. One suspect was dead. That left only Robert, who was officially just a person of interest at this point.

"I'll grab Michael," Daniel said. She took the moment alone to collect her thoughts.

Jesse suddenly turns up dead. Is it possible that Robert is behind this? Lanier left the building and waited outside the station for Daniel and Michael. *Is he back in New Orleans*?

They rode together to the crime scene.

"I find this rather convenient that Jesse's dead," Lanier said. "He must have made someone very angry."

Daniel nodded in agreement.

"What are your thoughts, Michael?" she asked.

"I don't really know what to think right now," he responded. "Jesse dead...wow." His eyes looked a bit glazed over, as if he were still shocked by the news.

Lanier glanced at Daniel. "I didn't ask if it was a suicide. I guess we'll find out when we get there."

The moment they arrived, they had to navigate through police officers and the CSI team. She slipped on gloves, did a cursory review of the crime scene, then walked over to the coroner preparing Jesse's body for transport. "I'd like to see him."

He unzipped the black body bag.

Jesse had been shot several times. Once in the head and twice in the chest.

"This wasn't a suicide," Lanier said to Daniel.

"Naw, it wasn't."

"He wasn't shot in this car. Looks like Jesse met up with someone over there," she said. "Whoever it was shot him. They either panicked or thought he was dead, but he wasn't. Jesse managed to drag himself back to his car. He got in and died there."

"Most likely bled out," Daniel said.

"He was shot close range," Michael interjected, pointing. "Over there under the bridge. Tire tracks...there was another car parked here."

They moved out of the way so the CSI techs could do their job.

She stopped a tech and asked, "Did anyone make a cast of the tracks?"

"We did."

"I'll make the notification to his mother," Michael said with a sigh. "The news of his death should come from me. I'll have one of the officers take me over there."

Lanier pulled Daniel off to the side. "I have a feeling that Robert may be back in New Orleans."

"Why do you say that?" he asked.

"The two men didn't like each other. All evidence points to Jesse, and now he turns up dead... Robert either killed him or had him murdered to keep him from talking to us."

"Jesse was the person who most likely almost ran you down—I'm sure he was the one behind your car accident, too," Daniel stated. "I can't prove it because we haven't been able to find the SUV, but I'm willing to bet he was behind the wheel. Maybe he's the person we've been looking for all along."

"My theory is that Jesse was killed to keep him from revealing the identity of the Crescent City Strangler. He was working for Robert and now he's dead."

"I really hope you're wrong about this."

Lanier met his gaze. "I don't believe I am. I trust my gut."

They watched a tech process Jesse's vehicle and its contents. The driver's seat was stained with blood. While the tech was taking photographs of the exterior, Lanier examined the interior. She found a lock box underneath the front passenger seat. Lanier took photos of it with her phone. "We need to get this open."

Daniel and another technician were able to unlock the box.

The tech began photographing the interior, including the ignition, the dash, glove box and rear seat area.

"Lanier, look at this," he said.

She joined him, her mouth dropping open in surprise. "Is this what I think it is?"

He nodded. "Souvenirs from the victims, including the wedding bands from the current vics. Jesse's the Crescent City Strangler."

Daniel sounded triumphant, but Lanier asked, "Why was he killed, then?" She still felt deep down that Robert was somehow connected to the murders. *This is just a little too easy.*

"Maybe he tried to attack another woman and she shot him," he responded. "They found some lipstick and some other stuff near the tracks of the other car."

"Where is the woman? Did she just drive away or

have someone pick her up? Why wouldn't she call the police? Especially if she shot him in self-defense."

"What do you think happened?"

"I don't believe that Jesse's the Crescent City Strangler," she responded. "My instincts tell me that Robert is the serial killer and he's here in New Orleans."

"I really hope you're wrong. I don't know what this would do to Michael."

"Your partner can barely stand the man," Lanier said.

"It's still his father. The media would have a field day with this—Michael and his kids would be dragged into it."

"Daniel, it's going to get out one way or the other. I feel bad for Michael, but he won't be blamed for his father's sins."

"We have no proof that Robert has ever been involved. It's only speculation. Items belonging to the victims were in this car. The evidence points to Jesse Miller."

"We both know that Robert lied to the police about Jesse being with him. Why would he do that? My gut tells me he was involved in this somehow, even if he was helping Jesse cover up his crimes."

"It's possible Jesse threatened him. Remember, he told us that Robert owed him for all the times he protected him when they were in reformatory school. Also, Jesse is the one who frequented the bars and had done so for years. No one ever recalled seeing Robert anywhere near Algiers Point and Tremé. The truth is, I'm glad it's not Michael's father."

Lanier sighed in resignation.

"Look, I know you're disappointed, but the reality is that we don't have anything to prove that Robert was ever involved in any crime. The only evidence we have is that he was a serial cheater. That doesn't make him a killer."

"You're right," Lanier responded.

"We should be celebrating tonight."

"What do you have in mind?" she asked.

"Dinner with me?"

She gave a slight nod. "Sure."

She knew Daniel thought the case had been solved, but Lanier wasn't so sure.

She had mixed feelings about the case coming to an end. It meant that Lanier would have to leave town soon.

Lanier suddenly felt a certain sadness at the thought because she wasn't ready to bid farewell to New Orleans. She wasn't ready to say goodbye to Daniel.

Chapter Twenty-One

Lanier couldn't shake the idea that they'd missed something, but she couldn't figure out what it could be. She'd lingered on it all morning. She glanced down at the stack of files on her desk, mentally checking items off her list.

She caught Daniel staring and gazed at him with brown eyes surrounded by long lashes. A faint smile graced her face as she tilted her head, asking, "Okay, what are you thinking?"

"How I wished we'd met outside of this job. Years ago, I got involved with a coworker. I almost lost my life over her."

That gave her pause. "What happened?"

"I became distracted," Daniel stated. "We were on the scene of a shoot-out, and I was so worried about her, I put myself in the line of danger. I was shot."

She let that sink in slowly. "You must have really loved her."

"I did, but in the end, the relationship didn't work out. It turns out that we didn't really want the same things. She wasn't interested in settling down. She preferred law enforcement to being a wife and motherhood."

"I know a few women like that," Lanier responded.

"What about you?" Daniel asked. "Have you thought about having a family?"

"Oh, I definitely want a husband and children," she said. "Right now, I travel a lot." Deep down, what she feared most was opening her heart fully after losing the two most important people in her life at such a young age.

"I admire your honesty," Daniel said. "It's a rare quality I see in people."

Lanier suddenly felt compelled to confess the secret she'd been keeping. "Speaking of honesty, I need to tell you something."

"What is it?"

"I was born in New Orleans and lived here until I was six years old. I had to move away because I lost my mother, then my grandmother six months later."

"Why didn't you say something before now?" Daniel asked.

"Because my mother is Gayle Giraud," Lanier announced.

Stunned, he sat up straight in his chair. "Is this why you're so determined to solve these cases? Are you out for revenge?"

"I want justice, Daniel. The same as *you*."

"You're too close to this, Lanier. You shouldn't have been a part of this investigation."

"I wouldn't be doing this if the previous task force hadn't given up so easily," Lanier stated. "I'm asking you to keep quiet about this. Please…"

Daniel gave a slight nod. "We've already found our killer. No harm has been done."

* * *

"What's this place?" Daniel asked.

"This is where I lived until I was six years old," Lanier responded. "The house belonged to my grandmother. My aunt owns the property now."

She pointed to the rusty bicycle leaning against the house. "My grandmother used to walk to the park while I rode that bike. I loved it." She paused for a heartbeat, then said, "I was here the day the police made notification of my mother's death." Her eyes grew wet with tears. "That was the worst day of my life."

"I can only imagine." Daniel embraced her. "My mother pretty much said the same thing when my dad died and the day I was shot."

"That was only the first heartbreak for me. Losing my grandmother six months later—I was traumatized. My aunt and uncle placed me in therapy for the first two years I lived with them."

"It must've helped. You accomplished quite a bit at a young age."

"I was focused. That's what kept me from losing myself. I knew back then I wanted to be in law enforcement, so I took karate and other self-defense classes. I figured no one would take me seriously unless I proved I could hold my own. I didn't want to be sitting behind a desk. I wanted to be in the field."

"I'm glad it's over for all of us," Daniel said.

"So am I."

"You don't look too happy about it, Lanier."

She uttered, "There was no justice in Jesse dying. If he's guilty, then he deserved to rot behind bars."

Back inside the car, Lanier asked, "How is Michael really holding up?"

"He didn't say much when he returned to the station, but for the most part, I think he was relieved that it wasn't Robert."

"I feel horrible for him."

"I hope you're right about this, Lanier," Daniel said.

"I trust my instincts. Robert Durousseau is going to come out of hiding sooner or later."

Daniel's phone began to vibrate just as the music playing on the radio was interrupted by a news report. Lanier turned up the volume. They were talking about the Durousseau estate. A body had been found under the floorboards in the guesthouse.

His phone vibrated once more. Daniel answered.

"Michael, I just heard on the news…"

"Do they know who it could be?" Lanier questioned.

He didn't respond to her because he was still talking to his partner. "No, you stay with the kids. I'll call you once I get there."

When Daniel hung up, she asked, "Is it the body of a woman?"

"No, they said it was a man."

Lanier looked at Daniel. "Surely they don't think it's Robert. Because if he's been dead all this time—who's been emailing Michael, and who killed the last four victims and attacked Abra?" Shaking her head, she said, "This isn't making any sense."

"If Robert is dead, then he couldn't have killed Jesse," Daniel responded.

"We need to go to the guesthouse."

"We're heading there now," Daniel said.

* * *

Once again, Lanier watched the CSI team carefully gather evidence to avoid contamination. Because the body had been interred beneath the flooring for years, they took mineralized dental plaque, and soil samples from the grave and from around the skeleton to help determine how long it had been there. The lab techs would conduct a CT scan to help build a digital image and help identify the remains.

"Robert disappeared…and maybe this is why?" she said. "Maybe he killed this man. Didn't a police officer disappear around that time, too?"

"I think you're right," Daniel responded. "I remember my parents talking about it. They never found the body. Some people thought he was the Crescent City Strangler, but all his alibis checked out. Maybe the officer confronted Robert because he discovered the truth and was murdered."

"Or maybe someone killed Robert and buried him in the spot where he killed all these women," Lanier offered. "Think about it… Jesse could've murdered Robert. Maybe he's the one who's been sending the emails to Michael. They were in reformatory school together. Jesse knew his employer well—I imagine he also knew some of Robert's secrets. Maybe that's what got him killed."

"And if the body is Robert?" Daniel asked.

Lanier didn't have an answer for him. She honestly didn't know what to think at this point.

Daniel turned around to see Michael walking briskly toward them. He met him halfway.

"Hey. I told you to stay home."

"I couldn't."

"Michael, I don't know what to say…"

"I've been a cop almost nine years, and for the first time I'm completely at a loss for words." His voice broke as he spoke. "When I was told a body was found, I thought maybe it was a woman… I told myself everything we've been thinking was true about Robert." He paused a moment, shaking his head. "That body has been there a really long time," Michael said. "The same original flooring. I used to hang out in the guesthouse with my friends… This is insane."

"So you don't think it's your father?"

Michael shook his head. "No. Robert is alive and hiding somewhere. Those emails are definitely from my father—they sound just like him."

Daniel felt bad for his partner. He could see the confusion and heartache etched on Michael's face.

"I really don't think that corpse is Robert. *It can't be.*" Although Michael appeared to be trying to keep his facial expression devoid of emotion, he was failing miserably.

Lanier and Daniel walked over to the main house to meet with Wilbur and Mary Denton, the current owners of the estate once owned by Robert Durousseau.

"This place is huge," she murmured.

The former estate of Robert Durousseau was considered the most coveted home in the Audubon Park neighborhood of New Orleans. Lanier agreed with the statement. The heavily fenestrated stucco abode featured a recessed entrance with an arched doorway.

The housekeeper ushered them into the home, where

they were greeted by a stunning chandelier, high ceilings and glossy hardwood floors in the central foyer.

They followed her past the kitchen with exposed brick walls and marble waterfall countertops to the sunroom.

Lanier enjoyed the breathtaking, unobstructed views of the patio, swimming pool and private lagoon. She even glimpsed the back of the guesthouse, which was separated from the house by the lagoon and live oaks. She knew Michael's family was wealthy, but she'd had no idea he'd grown up in a place like this. "I wonder why Michael decided to sell his family home?" she questioned. "It's so beautiful."

"He told me he didn't need a home this size. If you noticed, Michael's not the showy type. This guesthouse alone is bigger than my place. I think he said it has three bedrooms."

"Did you see the size of that office?"

Daniel nodded as Wilbur and his wife appeared before them.

"Thank you for agreeing to speak with us," Daniel stated.

"It's not a problem," he responded. "My wife and I don't know much, but we'll tell you what we do know."

He and Mary sat down on the sofa facing them. His wife seemed extremely nervous. Mary kept clutching and unclutching the folds of her dress. She didn't seem to know what to do with her hands. "How did you come to find the body?"

"My wife received an anonymous call," Wilbur responded. "I dismissed it as some sort of sick joke, but Mary wanted to be sure."

"It was the caller," his wife interjected. "He sounded desperate and angry. He said it was important the police knew about this body, then hung up. I felt a chill deep to my bones. I just knew he was telling the truth." Mary rubbed her arms as if she were cold even now. "I no longer want to live here."

"Honey…" Her husband patted her hand.

"No, I'm sorry. I feel as if I'm going to be sick," she muttered before running off.

"My apologies," Wilbur said. "My wife is fragile. This has been very traumatic for her. She's already talking about selling the house."

"I can imagine," Lanier said. "I'm really sorry you're having to deal with this."

"All this time we've been living here…we love our home. We raised our children here. Family members and friends have stayed in that guesthouse. We wouldn't have known anything if we hadn't gotten that phone call."

They asked a few more questions, and when they were out of the house, Lanier said, "That poor woman. It would certainly be unsettling for me to find out I've been living with some human remains under the floor."

Daniel had to agree. "In all my years, I've only had one case where there was a body discovered in the wall of a building. I think I'd been on the force a couple of years. Michael and I were the first responders."

"The world is filled with cruel people," Lanier uttered.

"At least one of them is dead. The world is safer from Jesse Miller tonight."

"I hope you're right," Lanier said. "But my gut tells me this is far from over."

Chapter Twenty-Two

Two days later, the remains were positively identified as those of Robert Durousseau.

Daniel wanted to be the one to tell Michael, but Lanier accompanied him into his partner's office. "The identity has been confirmed. It's your father," he said gently, placing a hand on Michael's shoulder. "The medical examiner identified him through his dental records."

Lanier glanced over at Michael. "I'm so sorry."

"Are they sure?" Michael asked thickly.

Daniel nodded. "It's him."

"So…so he's been dead all this time…" Michael suddenly excused himself and rushed out, but not before Daniel glimpsed the pain that flickered on his partner's face. He wanted to go after his friend, but he felt Michael needed this time to process his father's death alone.

"He's taking this news much harder than I thought he would," Lanier said quietly.

"Yeah. I feel helpless right now." He looked directly at her. "Robert's been dead for twenty years, so can we assume it was Jesse who was sending emails to Michael all this time?"

"The only thing about that theory is, I don't think he was that tech-savvy. The sender used a VPN and proxy servers. It's a foolproof method for masking an IP address when sending emails or doing anything else online."

"Apparently, he was a lot smarter than we thought or maybe someone else was helping him."

"All I can think about is poor Michael," Daniel said. "I plan to go by his house later to check on him."

"I think that's a good idea," Lanier stated. "He's going to need a friend right now."

Lanier sat in her office with the door closed. She was disappointed that with both Jesse and Robert dead, she wouldn't be able to get justice for her mother and the other women. A more fitting punishment would've been for the murderer to waste away in prison. As far as she was concerned, death was much too easy for them.

Her eyes filled, and she angrily swiped at them with her hand. Now wasn't the time or place to become emotional.

Lanier was frustrated because she still hadn't found the answers she sought.

Was Robert the Crescent City Strangler, or was it Jesse, as Daniel believed? Or was there a third person involved?

Daniel was going to be with Michael this evening, so when Sarah called and invited her over, she accepted. She needed a distraction after today, and she suddenly missed Aunt June and Celine terribly.

That evening after work, Lanier went straight to Sarah's house, where they sat in front of the fireplace and talked.

"I have so many questions about Robert Durousseau and Jesse Miller, but I'll hold them until the press conference."

Lanier awarded her a grateful smile. "Thanks, Sarah. Tonight, I just want to relax and not think about work at all."

Her phone rang. She looked at the caller ID and sighed. "I need to take this."

Sarah got up. "I'll give you some privacy."

When Sarah returned ten minutes later, Lanier announced, "That was my supervisor. I have to return to Virginia at the end of the week. It's time for me to go home."

"When are you going to tell Daniel?"

"I guess it'll have to be tomorrow."

Sarah sank down beside Lanier on the sofa. "I hope you don't mind my saying so, but you don't look at all happy about going back to Virginia."

"I love New Orleans. It was beginning to feel like home to me."

"And Daniel? How does he fit into this?" asked Sarah.

She gave a slight shrug. "I don't want a long-distance relationship. I'll never forget Daniel, but we don't have a future together."

"Are you sure about this?"

Shaking her head, Lanier said, "I'm not sure about anything." She'd known this day was coming, but she hadn't expected it to happen so soon. The investigation had come to an end as far as the bureau and the First Precinct were concerned. They had a name for their killer and could finally close the cold cases. The hunt for the Crescent City Strangler had officially come to an end despite her theory that there could be another suspect.

"I don't think you should just give up on love," Sarah stated. "It doesn't come around very often, Lanier. Trust me when I say this."

Lanier sighed softly. "I've lost almost everyone I've loved. I can't go through that kind of pain again."

"I can't imagine what you've gone through, and I'm so sorry for your losses, but you can't close your heart to love."

"I haven't, Sarah. Not really." And as she said it, she hoped it was true.

"You've been quiet all day," Daniel said when he entered Lanier's office the next day. He only had a couple hours left on his shift, so he wanted to talk to her. "What's going on?"

"I have to go home," Lanier responded. "They need me on another case."

He closed the door to her office, then asked, "When do you have to leave?"

"I report back to the bureau on Monday," she said.

"I don't want you to leave," Daniel stated quietly.

Lanier didn't respond. She just stared at him. "We knew this wasn't going to be permanent."

Daniel nodded. "But I want you in my life. I care about you, Lanier."

"When...when did you come to this realization?"

"I've known for a while. I tried to stifle these feelings, but I couldn't." He looked her straight in the eye. "I need to know if you feel anything for me, because I think you do. I think you have feelings for me, too."

"I care a great deal, Daniel. But I live in Alexandria. It wouldn't work." Lanier stood up and walked over to the window.

He stepped behind her, wrapping his arms around her.

She turned to face him. "I'm not denying I have feelings for you, Daniel… The reality is that I haven't had faith in anything for a long time. Including relationships."

"So you're willing to just give up on us without a fight?"

"You're a good man, Daniel. I'm not like you. I don't see life the same as you. We're too different, especially when it comes to faith in God. I have none."

"I know you feel that God abandoned you, but He hasn't."

"I don't agree. Eventually, this will become a problem. I really care about you, but I'm not the right woman for you."

"You're wrong. We're both committed to seeking justice for those who can't get it for themselves. We have a lot in common."

"I'm going back to Virginia on Saturday." She pasted on a smile as she stepped out of his embrace. "It was a pleasure working with you, Daniel."

"I thought you weren't leaving until this case was closed. You mentioned the possibility of a third suspect."

"I don't have any real evidence. Your boss told mine that we found our killers—Robert Durousseau and Jesse Miller. The case is closed. There will be things to process and statements to make to the public, but my job here is done," she said with a shrug.

"I never figured you for a quitter."

"This is for the best. You know if we're honest with ourselves, we'd have to admit that a relationship isn't going to work out between us. I don't believe in long distance, and you don't get involved with people you work with." Lanier faced him, getting lost in the depth of his eyes. She knew now what emotion she had glimpsed in his eyes earlier, the deep affection Daniel had for her.

He leaned in and kissed her delicately on the lips. "I'm not giving up on us." Both pulled away, though the sweetness of his touch lingered on her lips. As he walked away, Lanier wondered if she was doing the right thing.

Chapter Twenty-Three

As soon as Lanier entered her hotel suite, a strange sensation overtook her. Her gaze quickly assessed the interior, and a flicker of a shadow caught her eye.

She pulled out her gun, aiming it toward the bedroom just as Michael strolled out with his hands up.

"I'm not here to hurt you, Lanier. I just came to talk."

She dropped her arm to her side, but she didn't holster her weapon. It remained in her hand. "What are you doing in my room? You could've waited for me in the lobby."

"I told you," Michael responded. "I came to talk to you."

"About what?"

"Robert."

"What's so important about your father that you had to break into my suite?"

"I wanted to apologize to you."

Lanier met his gaze. *"For what?"*

"He killed your mother," Michael stated without preamble.

When she didn't respond, he continued, "I knew there

was something familiar about you the moment you arrived at the station, but it wasn't until I saw the way you looked at Gayle Giraud's photos—that's when I realized who you really are. You have your mother's eyes and her beautiful smile." He grinned. "I'm very happy to meet you. Gayle used to talk about you all the time. I often wondered how you were doing. You should know your mother loved you so much…"

"How long have you known that Robert was the Crescent City Strangler?" she questioned, cutting him off. "You seemed surprised when I first asked you about him, but there was something in your eyes. I couldn't figure it out until now. You *knew* all along that you were the son of a serial killer."

"Since I was fifteen." Michael seemed to be studying her face, as if trying to gauge her reaction.

"How did you find out?"

"It was purely by accident. Robert…he had a thing for prostitutes," Michael stated. "He often brought them to the guesthouse late at night. A few days after my fifteenth birthday, I witnessed my father killing this one stripper. He saw me and gestured for me to come inside."

"How did it make you feel?" Lanier asked.

"I was afraid at first, but my dad—he told me that she wasn't worth keeping alive another day. Robert said she was just one of many dirty women in this world. He drilled that into my head repeatedly. Then a month later, he woke me up one night, told me to get dressed, and took me out with him. We picked up a prostitute, and she paid for her wanton behavior with her life."

"When did you make your first kill, Michael?"

He met her gaze. "On my sixteenth birthday. Robert showed me exactly how to grab them by the neck to bring about death, but I found it easier to strangle them with rope. Robert was pleased with my idea to use the rope. He said changing the MO would keep the police guessing. And it did. For the first time in my life, Robert was proud of me."

Lanier swallowed the wave of disgust she felt flowing through her. Michael actually felt a sense of pride and accomplishment in what he'd done.

"When I was nineteen, my mother found the photos and souvenirs we kept. She was repulsed, but the way she looked at me—it was my undoing. She called us murderers—said we sickened her. She then took her life, right there in front of us. Robert made me pick up the souvenirs off the floor and find a new hiding place."

"Why my mother?" Lanier asked without preamble. "Why did he kill her?"

"I'm afraid I'm to blame for Gayle's death."

"What do you mean?"

"I met your mother when I was twenty-one at the bar where she worked. Jesse and I used to hang out there on the weekends. Your mom was twenty-four at the time, but she was always nice to me. I could tell she was different from the other women there, but I knew my father wouldn't approve. Only Jesse knew about our friendship."

"So what happened?" Lanier pressed.

"Robert followed me one night to the bar. I was walking Gayle to her car when he confronted us. We got into a terrible argument, and he killed her to show me he was one who was truly in control. Gayle was the only woman I ever loved. She was sweet and innocent. She didn't deserve to die."

"Did she love you?" Lanier asked. Deep down, she'd

never believe her mother could love the man standing before her.

She relaxed when Michael responded, "No, your mother viewed me as nothing more than a friend."

"And you just let your father kill her," she hissed. "You did nothing to try to save her."

"I punished him. Robert begged for his life, but I didn't care. I also wanted him dead because of the responsibility placed on my shoulders by a father who was a killer." His eyes became dark and insolent. "Can't you see that I'm the real victim here?"

"What was Jesse Miller's part in all this?"

"I guess you can say he was an unwilling participant."

"How so?"

"Jesse came to the estate with the intent to avenge Anna's death. I don't know what he meant to do, but he walked into the guesthouse with a knife right after I'd shot Robert. I convinced Jesse to help me bury him under the floor. I later had them completely redone before I sold the home. This year, I needed his help again. He was reluctant until I convinced Jesse that I had enough evidence to frame him for all the murders." Michael paused a moment, then said, "I'd suspected he was up to something, so I got rid of him. I had everything in place for him to be blamed. Jesse had the last word, though. He was the anonymous caller, and now here we are."

Lanier stared boldly at Michael. "Why are you telling me all this?"

"So you understand that you and I are both victims," he said, almost desperately.

"I don't see it that way at all," she responded. "Those

women…my mother…*they* are the *victims*. You are a murderer just like your father. I do have some questions I'd like you to answer."

"That's why I'm here."

"I'd like to know who was watching me that night at the hotel. You or Jesse?"

"That was me," Michael responded without further explanation.

"The phone call?" Lanier asked.

"Me."

"The car accident and someone nearly running me down?"

"That was Jesse, but at my instruction."

"Why?"

"I'd hoped to discourage you from investigating any further. For the record, I felt regret for my actions after learning you were Gayle's daughter."

"Michael, you didn't have to be like Robert. You could've said no."

Shaking his head, he said, "No was not an option for that man. When I took his life—that's when I was finally free. I was able to control my urges until Carly broke our marriage vows. She started hanging out at bars with her friends, and then she got involved with some dude. I followed her one night to his place."

"Is he still breathing?"

"I blamed her—we said vows. She was the one I took issue with, so I punished her. And then I punished those other four women for breaking their vows. I tried to punish Abra… She was a fighter."

As Lanier listened to Michael, she realized in horror

that there was another victim they hadn't been aware of. *"You murdered your wife."*

Daniel headed to the hotel. He had to talk to Lanier. "I'm not giving up on us," he whispered.

He walked briskly through the lobby, walking briskly toward the elevator.

Rubbing the area between his brows, Daniel closed his eyes. He'd taken his shot at being honest with Lanier, and she'd given her response. He'd tried but couldn't get her to change her mind.

Did I really try hard enough?

The question nagged at him.

Daniel practiced his argument as he stepped off the elevator and made his way to Lanier's hotel room.

He was about to knock when he heard her say, "You murdered your wife…"

"Lanier, I didn't come here to talk about that unfaithful tramp—only to give you the answer you were searching for," Michael said. "You deserved to know what happened to your mother. I wanted to give you closure. I wanted you to know the truth, and I guess I needed to unburden myself."

Daniel's heart throbbed in his ears. He couldn't believe it was his partner in there with Lanier. It took him a moment to comprehend what Michael was saying.

Carly didn't just pack up and leave. He killed her.

"And what did you expect me to do with this information?" Lanier was asking. "I'm not just going to let you walk away."

"You got what you came here for. Just leave and never come back to New Orleans."

"Michael, you may not have killed my mother, but you've murdered other innocent women."

"I'm giving you a chance to just walk away."

"You know it doesn't work that way," Lanier uttered. "You wanted to be caught. That's why you confessed to me."

"I wasn't confessing. I simply told you what happened."

"Call it whatever you want, Michael, but you're not leaving this room a free man," Lanier stated. "I'm afraid I can't let that happen."

"It galls you that you were wrong, doesn't it?" he taunted. "You came so close, but you still didn't have all the information."

Anger burned through Daniel at the thought of Lanier being in danger. He had to find a way to save her. A tight pressure straddled his shoulders. He didn't have time to consider a plan of action any longer but resisted the urge to break down the door.

Just then, Daniel spotted one of the housekeepers and said, "It's imperative that I get into this room."

"You need to speak with the manager," she responded.

Something fleshly rose inside Daniel. He suddenly wanted nothing more than to project all his rage onto Michael, the man who'd betrayed his trust and presented a threat to Lanier.

Showing his badge, Daniel said, "I don't have time to speak with your manager. I also need you to call the police. The woman in that suite is in danger."

Lanier's instincts forewarned her that this current situation would not go well.

What if I never see Daniel again? She regretted the way they'd left things between them.

Suddenly, the door to the suite blew open, catching both her and Michael off guard.

Before Lanier could react, Michael quickly grabbed her, placing his gun to her head. "Drop your gun," he ordered.

She did as he instructed.

"You too, Daniel."

"No need to hurt her," he said calmly, his weapon trained on his partner. "It'll only make things worse for you."

"I mean it. Drop the gun," Michael stated. "I'll kill Lanier. At this point, I don't have anything to lose."

"Think about your children."

"I'm not gonna say it again, Daniel. Throw your gun to the floor and kick it over here."

"Let Lanier go."

A crazed look on his face, Michael pulled the trigger.

Lanier squeezed her eyes shut.

Father God, please help me…

When she opened them again, both she and Michael looked shocked.

The bullet had jammed inside the barrel.

Lanier glanced at Daniel before impulsively dropping to the floor, enabling him to get off a shot, which slammed into Michael's shoulder.

He flinched in pain, dropping his gun. "I'm gonna kill you…"

The barely contained rage in Michael's words shifted her adrenaline to overdrive. Lanier saw his fist swing out, trying to strike her, and backed out of his reach. She kicked his weapon out of his range.

Feeling a white-hot fury like she'd never known before, Lanier lunged at Michael, using her full strength and body weight, knocking him to the floor. Blood spread across the carpet from the gunshot wound in his shoulder.

His body jerked, and he growled in pain. She didn't care. Lanier punched him in the face, then quickly picked up her gun and pressed it to his head. "I should put an end to your miserable life right now," she uttered.

Michael moaned again.

Daniel pulled her off so he could subdue Michael with handcuffs, all the while reciting the Miranda rights. "You have the right to remain silent. If you do say anything, what you say can be used against you in a court of law…"

"I know my rights," Michael interjected.

In the distance, they could hear sirens.

Michael sat in the middle of the floor with his hands secured behind his back, scowling at her.

While they waited for the police officers and paramedics to arrive, Lanier said, "It's over for you. So, why don't you tell me where your wife is buried?"

He didn't respond.

"How could you murder the mother of your children?" Daniel asked. "How can you ever explain this to them? Did you even think of them?"

Silence.

Lanier shook her head, unable to stop staring at Michael, knowing he'd intended to kill her. Full-on anger coursed through her veins. "Your father may have been the Crescent City Strangler, but you're no better than he was. You're just as coldhearted and callous. Your children will be better off without you. Hopefully you haven't poisoned them as Robert did you."

Michael glared at her, pure hatred in his eyes. "You never should've come back here. I promise you one day you will regret it."

"That's not likely," Lanier responded. "It's just as unlikely you'll ever see the outside of a prison again."

"I have ways of getting to you."

She walked over to him and uttered, *"Bring it."*

If Michael thought she'd show fear, he had never been so wrong. Lanier wasn't afraid of him.

Chapter Twenty-Four

Numb, Daniel left the interrogation room. He walked past his desk and went outside.

Lanier followed him to a nearby bench, where he sat.

"This certainly didn't turn out the way I expected," she said quietly, taking a seat beside him. "You were right, Daniel. We were dealing with two murderers and an accomplice. Robert trained his own son to be a serial killer. Then Michael blackmailed Jesse into helping him cover his tracks when he started killing again."

"All these years I've worked with Michael... I had no idea."

"His wife's infidelity is what triggered him, so he targeted women who were unfaithful. He killed Carly but made sure no one knew she was dead. Michael didn't want her body to be found."

"Because he would've been our first suspect," Daniel said.

"No, it's more than that," Lanier responded. "It's his way of getting revenge. Michael is punishing Carly by having her spend eternity in some unmarked grave—probably deep in the swamps."

"I never thought him a cruel man, but the way he looked earlier—it was pure evil."

"I'm so sorry, Daniel. I know he was your friend."

He shrugged. "Apparently, I never knew Michael at all. That's the truth of it." Daniel touched her cheek. "I couldn't bear it if something had happened to you." He wanted to say so much more, but he didn't have the emotional capacity to do so.

Lanier kissed him, her lips communicating all the emotions Daniel was besieged with himself. "Why don't you go home?"

"I think I will," he said after a moment.

"Is there anything I can do for you?" she asked.

Daniel shook his head. "I'll be fine. I just need some time alone."

"If you feel up to talking, call me," Lanier said.

They stood up and embraced.

She watched him walk to his car and get inside. Daniel waved, then pulled out of the parking space.

Fifteen minutes later, he walked into his house and went straight to his bedroom. It had been a long night, and tomorrow would be even longer. There was a lot of paperwork to do. The cold cases could now be closed. He could close the current ones as well. However, they would have to open a new case for Carly Durousseau. Daniel hoped to convince Michael to tell them where he buried her body.

A lone tear rolled down his cheek as he thought about his partner—the man he called friend for many years. Anger coursed through his body as Michael's betrayal stung. Daniel had taken him into his confidence. All this time they had been looking for the serial killer…oh how Michael must have laughed at them.

How could I not know that the man was a murderer? Why didn't I see it?

Lanier did not sleep well that night, despite Michael's capture. She didn't feel avenged—only sad. The innocent faces of his children stayed at the forefront of her mind. Michael had acted out what must have been initially unthinkable, but he eventually became a willing participant. He chose to follow his father's path.

When Lanier eventually drifted off to sleep, she was jerked awake by a dream in which Michael had shot her in the head. She sat up in bed, her top damp from perspiration.

Lanier climbed out of bed and padded barefoot to the bathroom to wash her face and change her shirt. When she returned to bed, she climbed in and tried to go back to sleep, but it eluded her for hours.

After an hour passed and another, Lanier sat up and tried reading, but gave up after about thirty minutes.

For the first time in years, she went down on her knees to pray. She knew without a doubt that it was God who'd saved her life, and Lanier was extremely grateful. She prayed in earnest; her faith renewed.

She plumped up her pillows and tried to fall asleep once more, this time succeeding.

The alarm went off at seven o'clock.

Lanier sat up, groaning, and eased her way out of bed. The cold that came over her when she threw the blankets off awakened her senses, forcing her to turn up the heat a notch. When it was warm enough, Lanier showered and dressed for work.

She passed on eating breakfast because she didn't have an appetite. Instead, she headed straight to the station.

The solemn mood there matched her own. Everyone was shocked that Michael was the serial killer they had been looking for—it was the ultimate betrayal.

"Good morning," Daniel greeted her dismally.

She accepted the cup of coffee he offered. "Morning... I really didn't know if I'd see you today."

"I have a lot of paperwork to do." Looking at her, he asked, "Are you okay?"

Lanier stared at the empty desk where Michael used to sit. "Not really. Last night, I didn't sleep well. I kept thinking about his children and what will happen to them."

"His cousin Ruby offered to have them come live with her. Understandably, everyone is in shock right now."

She nodded. "Normally I can sense danger, but with Michael, there was nothing. I actually felt bad for him—having to raise two kids alone. He fooled us all."

"Me most of all," Daniel stated.

Although he tried to hide his disappointment and sadness, he was unable to do so successfully. Lanier could see the pain etched in his expression.

Lanier was grateful that her mother's murder, along with the others, had finally been solved, but a part of her heart was broken for Daniel. She wanted to comfort him, but that would have to wait until they were alone.

"It pains me to see you this way. I'm really sorry, Daniel."

"None of this is your fault, Lanier." He shook his

head. "I'm meeting with Sarah in about thirty minutes. I promised I'd give her an exclusive."

"Michael's name will be run through the mud, and he deserves it," Lanier stated. "I don't feel bad for him at all."

"The one thing I can't forget is when Michael put the gun to my head," Lanier stated later, when they left the police station to have lunch. "I just knew I was about to die. But then the gun jammed… It was as if someone stopped it. The reason I say that is because it fired with no problem in the lab. The ammo wasn't faulty."

"It's hard to explain in the natural," Daniel said. "What I believe is that God protected you. He did it in a way so you'd know it could only be Him."

"It would seem so," she responded. "I can't get over it. Why would He save me and not those other women?"

"Apparently, your work isn't done, Lanier."

She pondered his words while they ate. Daniel was right. If the ammunition had been found faulty, she would've easily attributed what happened to that.

Lanier realized that God had also answered her prayer for justice. Everything she'd gone through and accomplished had not been on her own.

"I've just realized that God has been with me all this time, Daniel." Her eyes filled with tears as the weight of that hit her. "I'm so grateful."

Daniel patted her hand, and they sat for a moment in silence before they continued to eat.

"I have something I want to say to you," she stated after they finished the meal and were on their way out of the restaurant.

"What is it?" he asked.

"Meeting you…you've made me realize that I'm ready for something more in my life."

"I'm not sure where this is going…" Daniel said.

"You told me you care for me, and at the time I didn't respond, but I want you to know that I've fallen in love you. Since losing my mom and grandmother, I've been so afraid to open my heart to anyone." Lanier met his gaze. "I'm not scared anymore. I was born in New Orleans, and this will always be my home." She took his hand in her own. "Now that I'm back, I don't want to leave. I had a conversation with my supervisor this morning and told him that."

"I want you to stay…wait…does this mean you're transferring here?"

She smiled. "I put in a request. I'm not sure how long it'll take, but until then, I guess we'll have to travel back and forth. Now that the Crescent City Strangler is no longer a concern, I don't intend on staying with the bureau. My long-term goal is to go to law school here in New Orleans."

"Really?"

Lanier nodded. "It's time to move on. I'm not leaving law enforcement entirely. I'd like to be a district attorney—maybe even sit on the bench. I still intend to balance the scales of justice—only in the courtroom."

Lanier's words were music to his ears. She continued to amaze him. Daniel closed his eyes and sent up a quick prayer of gratitude for an answered prayer.

"Daniel…?" she prompted.

"You don't have any idea how happy you just made me." She was giving them a real chance—and he wouldn't squander it. He wanted to be with her.

She broke into a grin. "I'll still be with the FBI until I finish school. Are you going to be okay with that?"

"I can handle it." Working this case with her had taught him this was a risk worth taking. Besides, they wouldn't be working together anymore. He could date her and not worry about being distracted.

Joy consumed Daniel's heart as he gazed at her.

"What are you smiling about?" she asked.

"In that very moment, I got a glimpse of my future with you. It will be one filled with laughter and the kind of love that will last a lifetime."

Lanier placed a hand to his cheek. "I'm looking forward to whatever God has in store for us."

Epilogue

One year later

Daniel took Lanier to Café Dauphine in the ninth ward for a Réveillon dinner.

"You look beautiful," he told her. "I'm glad I was able to convince you to take a break from your studies. You're supposed to be on a break for the holidays."

"Thank you." She'd chosen a black mock turtleneck dress with a black-and-gold belt. Her black leather boots with gold trim matched perfectly. Every time Lanier looked at Daniel, her heart turned over in response. They had spent the last year dating and getting to know one another on a personal level. She still missed Celine and her aunt and uncle, but she felt at home in New Orleans. She and Daniel were renovating her childhood home and planned to use it as a rental property. Ever since Michael's conviction, a huge weight had been lifted from her. They'd finally gotten justice for her mother and all those other women.

She chose gumbo for her first course while he selected the crawfish corn chowder.

"This is sooo good," Lanier murmured.

"Do you want to try mine?"

"No, I need to leave room for the rest of my meal."

The second course consisted of fried green tomatoes and rémoulade salad.

When the third course of fried chicken was served, Daniel wiped his mouth, then said, "I can't believe it's almost Christmas."

"Me, too," Lanier responded. "I haven't even started shopping for gifts. I've been so busy with work and law school…"

"Don't stress yourself out, sweetheart. Just give gift cards. Everyone knows you're carrying a full plate right now."

She awarded him a warm smile. "Thank you, baby. I appreciate that you've been so supportive. It's nice to know that you believe in me."

"You never have to worry about that."

They chose the raisin-pecan bread pudding for the last course.

"This is so yummy," Lanier said. "I need to order some of this to go."

"And so we shall."

"The ambiance…the food…you—this night is so perfect, Daniel." She reached over, covering his hand with her own. "I'm so happy being here in New Orleans with you."

They finished off the dessert.

Settling back in her chair, Lanier said, "I don't know about you, but I'm stuffed. I'm glad we shared the dessert."

Daniel chuckled. "It was delicious, though."

She patted the to-go bag. "And we've got more for tomorrow night."

After they left the restaurant, Daniel took Lanier down to the lake, where several rustic, shack-like buildings served as boathouses.

She'd had no idea, but he'd arranged for a Venetian gondola ride around the lake as a surprise. "This is so beautiful at night," Lanier murmured as they drifted on the water. "This view is spectacular."

Seated beside her, Daniel said, "Sweetheart, I love you so much, and I want to spend the rest of my life with you."

Her eyebrows rose a notch at the sight of the tiny velvet box in his hand.

"Will you marry me?"

His proposal made Lanier gasp in surprise. "Is this for real?"

"Yeah." He laughed. "I want you to marry you. I'm happy you've finally relocated to New Orleans, but I want more—I want you to be my wife."

She hugged him. "I love you so much, Daniel."

"Then tell me if you're going to accept my proposal."

"Definitely," she responded. "I will marry you. You're the only man I want to have children with, grow old with... I see you as my best friend, my other half."

Daniel placed the ring on her finger—a two-karat cushion-cut emerald with channel-set diamonds on each side. "You mentioned how your mother always wanted an emerald engagement ring... When I saw this one, I knew it was perfect for you."

"I love it," she said with a grin. "Wow... I can't believe we're getting married. Sarah is going to have a fit when she finds out. She's been predicting this from the moment I met her."

"Well, she was right. And we will never hear the end of it. She's gonna be delighted by the news."

"Congratulations," the gondolier said.

"Thanks," Lanier murmured as she gazed at Daniel. This was the happiest, most perfect moment of her life. For the first time in a long time, all the shadows surrounding her heart had finally dissipated. She loved him with her heart, body and soul.

"My one request is that we have the second line parade," Lanier stated.

"It wouldn't be a New Orleans wedding if we didn't dance down the street with musicians," Daniel responded. "It signifies the beginning of a new life together. I can't wait to start our life together as man and wife."

Lanier took his hand in her own. "Neither can I."

* * * * *

Get 4 FREE REWARDS!

We'll send you 2 FREE Books plus 2 FREE Mystery Gifts.

FREE Value Over **$20**

Both the **Love Inspired**® and **Love Inspired**® **Suspense** series feature compelling novels filled with inspirational romance, faith, forgiveness, and hope.

YES! Please send me 2 FREE novels from the Love Inspired or Love Inspired Suspense series and my 2 FREE gifts (gifts are worth about $10 retail). After receiving them, if I don't wish to receive any more books, I can return the shipping statement marked "cancel." If I don't cancel, I will receive 6 brand-new Love Inspired Larger-Print books or Love Inspired Suspense Larger-Print books every month and be billed just $6.24 each in the U.S. or $6.49 each in Canada. That is a savings of at least 17% off the cover price. It's quite a bargain! Shipping and handling is just 50¢ per book in the U.S. and $1.25 per book in Canada.* I understand that accepting the 2 free books and gifts places me under no obligation to buy anything. I can always return a shipment and cancel at any time by calling the number below. The free books and gifts are mine to keep no matter what I decide.

Choose one: ☐ **Love Inspired**
Larger-Print
(122/322 IDN GRDF)

☐ **Love Inspired Suspense**
Larger-Print
(107/307 IDN GRDF)

Name (please print)

Address   Apt. #

City   State/Province   Zip/Postal Code

Email: Please check this box ☐ if you would like to receive newsletters and promotional emails from Harlequin Enterprises ULC and its affiliates. You can unsubscribe anytime.

Mail to the Harlequin Reader Service:
IN U.S.A.: P.O. Box 1341, Buffalo, NY 14240-8531
IN CANADA: P.O. Box 603, Fort Erie, Ontario L2A 5X3

Want to try 2 free books from another series! Call 1-800-873-8635 or visit www.ReaderService.com.

---

*Terms and prices subject to change without notice. Prices do not include sales taxes, which will be charged (if applicable) based on your state or country of residence. Canadian residents will be charged applicable taxes. Offer not valid in Quebec. This offer is limited to one order per household. Books received may not be as shown. Not valid for current subscribers to the Love Inspired or Love Inspired Suspense series. All orders subject to approval. Credit or debit balances in a customer's account(s) may be offset by any other outstanding balance owed by or to the customer. Please allow 4 to 6 weeks for delivery. Offer available while quantities last.

Your Privacy—Your information is being collected by Harlequin Enterprises ULC, operating as Harlequin Reader Service. For a complete summary of the information we collect, how we use this information and to whom it is disclosed, please visit our privacy notice located at corporate.harlequin.com/privacy-notice. From time to time we may also exchange your personal information with reputable third parties. If you wish to opt out of this sharing of your personal information, please visit readerservice.com/consumerschoice or call 1-800-873-8635. **Notice to California Residents**—Under California law, you have specific rights to control and access your data. For more information on these rights and how to exercise them, visit corporate.harlequin.com/california-privacy.

LIRLIS22R2

HARLEQUIN
PLUS

Announcing a **BRAND-NEW**
multimedia subscription service
for romance fans like you!

Read, Watch and Play.

Experience the easiest way to get
the romance content you crave.

Start your **FREE 7 DAY TRIAL** at
<u>www.harlequinplus.com/freetrial</u>.

IF YOU ENJOYED THIS BOOK, DON'T MISS NEW EXTENDED-LENGTH NOVELS FROM LOVE INSPIRED!

In addition to the Love Inspired books you know and love, we're excited to introduce even more uplifting stories in a longer format, with more inspiring fresh starts and page-turning thrills!

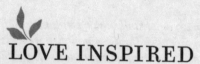

LOVE INSPIRED

Stories to uplift and inspire.

Fall in love with Love Inspired—inspirational and uplifting stories of faith and hope. Find strength and comfort in the bonds of friendship and community. Revel in the warmth of possibility, and the promise of new beginnings.

LOOK FOR THESE LOVE INSPIRED TITLES ONLINE AND IN THE BOOK DEPARTMENT OF YOUR FAVORITE RETAILER!

SPECIAL EXCERPT FROM

LOVE INSPIRED
INSPIRATIONAL ROMANCE

MOUNTAIN RESCUE

*When an arsonist stalks their small Colorado town,
Mike Byrne and Julia Beaumont flee with his young
daughter to a mountain cabin for safety. Only, the
arsonist is closer than they think and nowhere is safe.
Least of all the treacherous, snow-covered Rockies…*

Read on for a sneak preview of
Refuge Up in Flames
by New York Times *bestselling author Shirley Jump.*

"Oh, no," Mike whispered. "Not here, too."

A heavy stone of foreboding dropped in Julia's stomach as she slowly rose and pivoted to look at whatever Mike had just seen.

A fire was beginning to curl up the side of the cabin next door. It was maybe thirty yards away, separated by a dozen trees—and a pile of chopped wood that stretched between the cabins like one long dynamite fuse.

How could this have happened? There'd been no lightning. No one was staying in the other cabins. There was no reason a fire could spontaneously begin next door. There was only one answer—

The evil that had been setting Crooked Valley on fire had followed them here. Why?

"Daddy! There's a fire!" Ginny pointed at the orange flames eagerly running up the wooden siding of the cabin next door, inches away from the woodpile. Any hope Julia had that her eyes were deceiving her disappeared. The house next door was on fire, and their lives were suddenly in very real danger.

LIMREXP1022

"We need to get out of here. Now." Mike grabbed Ginny's coat and started helping her arms into the sleeves. Julia bent down beside him and fastened the zipper, then grabbed Ginny's hat and tugged it on her head as Mike pulled back on his boots. Julia grabbed her coat just in time to see the flames leap to the pile of dried wood and race across the top like a hungry animal.

Heading straight for their cabin.

"Get in my car!" Mike shouted.

They ran for the SUV, but Julia stopped short just as Mike opened the passenger-side door. "Mike, look." The two front tires had been slashed. Julia spun to the right and saw the same thing had been done to her car. "Someone doesn't want us leaving," she said under her breath. Fear curled a tight fist inside her chest.

Mike quickly scanned the area. "He's out there. Somewhere."

Oh, God. Why would the arsonist follow them? Why would he target Mike and Ginny? Or Julia, for that matter?

A chill snaked up her spine as she realized the arsonist must have *watched* them stringing lights, singing Christmas carols. He'd watched them—and still decided to take the lives of two adults and a small child. What kind of evil person did that?

"Come on. We have to go on foot." Mike took Julia's hand in one hand, then scooped up Ginny with the other.

Even as he said the words, she could see the fire overtaking the small cabin, eagerly devouring the Christmas lights they had just hung. The sweet moment the three of them had was being erased.

It was a two-mile trip down the mountain. Another two miles back to town. On foot, they'd never make it before dark. How were they going to get back to safety?

Don't miss
Refuge Up in Flames *by Shirley Jump,*
available December 2022 wherever
Love Inspired books and ebooks are sold.

LoveInspired.com

A collection of lost books holds the clues to her family's legacy...and her future

Don't miss this uplifting page-turner from

MOLLIE RUSHMEYER

"A warmhearted and bookish literary debut."
—**Lisa Wingate**, *New York Times* bestselling author

Available now from Love Inspired!

LOVE INSPIRED
LoveInspired.com